CW01288164

Self-portrait
by
John B. Keane

THE MERCIER PRESS
CORK

© J. B. Keane

ISBN 978-1-781-17911-6

TO
DICKEEN ROCHE

Transferred to Digital Print-on-Demand in 2024

CHAPTER

I

I was born on the 21st of July, 1928, in the town of Listowel, in County Kerry.

Apart from my birth, it was an uneventful year, free of plague, war and famine.

The Kuomintang was established at Pekin without my knowledge or consent. The Fifth Reform Act was passed in spite of me. The Kellog Peace Pact was signed in Paris, and all wars were condemned (until the next one). The first five-year plan was launched by Joe Stalin, and the Russians haven't stopped launching things since. In Ireland tobacco was one and fourpence a quarter pound and whiskey was tenpence a half-glass. Television was unknown. Radio was a luxury and gramophones with indecent appendages were the order of the day.

I weighed twelve pounds at birth, but Davy Lawlor, the parish clerk, assured my sponsors that chances of latter-day normality were fifty-fifty.

I was the fourth member of a family of five boys and four girls. I was christened plain John but assumed the 'B.' legitimately at Confirmation as a mark of respect to the late Brendan the Navigator, patron saint of the diocese of Kerry, proof, if any is needed, to buttress the contention that I am, indeed, a strong and perfect Christian.

For a while I was something of a problem to my parents because the power of speech escaped me until I was three years of age. When I started, however, I could not be stopped and since that time I cherish the belief that I have more than made up for my slow start.

My mother was a small-farmer's daughter from Ballydonoghue, a townland half-way between Listowel and Ballybunion. My father was a national teacher. Three of my grandparents exited before my entry to this world but the memory of my maternal grandmother is strong. She wore a red petticoat and came to Listowel in a donkey-and-car. She brought eggs at Easter and a turkey at Christmas. She was always good for tuppence. Her favourite song was *'Green Grows the Laurel and Soft Falls the Dew'* but it was from her that I picked up songs like *'The Sandhills of Kilmore'* and *'The Caves of Guhard'*, and also nonsensical but humorous frivolities like:

> *'Ere last night and the night before*
> *Three jackasses came to my door;*
> *One had a fiddle, one had a drum,*
> *And one had a pancake stuck to his bum…'*

I used to die laughing at this, although it brought disquieting notoriety when I was overheard repeating it by a virtuous lady of the neighbourhood, who's now passed on to her eternal reward, God rest her!

Shortly before I went to school another old lady who lived down the street used invite me into her house and ply me with pieces of rich cake and apple-pie. She would ask me what we had for our dinner that day and about whom my father and mother might be talking at dinner-time. I quickly entered the spirit of the thing and gave her the kind of answers she expected.

I remember my father vaguely during my first year at Listowel National School. I was four years of age then. I sat next to a fair-haired angel-faced boy who later served with distinction in the Palestine Police, with such distinction in fact that less than half of his body was recovered by his militant brethren. The old school was undergoing repairs in 1932 and all the classes occupied chalked-off spaces on the extensive first floor of the Carnegie Free Lbrary, which stood directly across the street from the school.

My father taught Fifth Grade, at the other end of the room from 'Low Infants'. Once or twice during the day he would cough. It was a very familiar cough and I usually managed to catch his eye immediately afterwards. He would wink an eye without changing his expression, and things always bucked up after that.

Frequently I would raise my hand for permission to go outside. My mother had instructed me somewhat forcefully in this respect. The toilet was on the ground floor and the only means of getting to it was down the fire escape, an expedition which always demanded the assistance of an older boy. One of my brothers was invariably chosen. Sometimes I was pushed around when they discovered, after failing to perform, that there was no necessity for the trip. 'Better be sure than sorry!' my father would always say when we got home.

When I passed into High Infants, my father left Listowel School for good and accepted the principalship of Clounmacon National School, three miles from Listowel. He could not afford a car and he could not remain on a bicycle for long, so for twenty years he walked the three miles out and the three miles back. I do not remember a single complaint. Hail, rain or shine, he seldom missed a day. I wrote him a poem a few years ago, which even he liked:

> '*I am terribly proud of my father,*
> *Bitterly, faithfully proud;*
> *Let none say a word to my father*
> *Or mention his name out loud.*
> *I adored his munificent blather*
> *Since I was his catch as catch can*
> *Let none say a word of my father*
> *For he was a lovable man.*'

My father introduced me to Sam Weller, Micawber, and other distinguished notables. It was years before I discovered that they weren't his personal friends at all although I am still convinced that Ben Gunn frequently sent us cheese and that Silver ended his days in Gurtenard, a delightful wood near Listowel.

Those early years at National School are hazy and dim and the unpleasant incidents, the deliberate cruelties of boys and teachers are best forgotten, but there is one teacher who still stands out very clearly. His name was Michael Keane. No relation!

He was the Principal Teacher of Listowel Boys' National School, Lower. He was a tall man with a very broad-brimmed hat and a fierce-looking moustache. He is dead for more than twenty years but his son, Michael, is now principal in the same school.

When a small boy committed a crime of national importance, he was sent to Michael Keane for punishment. There was no corridor and it was the long walk through other classrooms that took the guts out of a person. There were the sympathetic glances from other small boys who had run the gauntlet before. Then there was the final, the awful knocking at his door. He had two slappers – one round and one flat. The round one was made of bamboo. The flat one was for major crimes such as spilling inkwells and pinching neighbours. He smoked a turned-down pipe and when a small boy entered his sanctuary he brought the flat slapper to bear upon the palm of the hand. There was a resounding smack, very loud – like the discharge of a small calibre weapon. There was no pain whatsoever.

The flat slapper was merely a symbol.

When the punishment was over he generally gave a boy a penny and, if the boy was very small, a pull out of his pipe. On birthdays he arranged a collection – a box was passed from pupil to pupil and each contributed what he could. In the end the heterogeneous contents were presented to the lucky celebrant. No money found its way into the box, but there were marbles, tops, comics, sweets, stale buns, apples – sometimes half-eaten, nails, bottle-openers, nibs and, occasionally, a pencil-topper from some noble and generous soul who had grown tired of it and who would, maybe, demand it back again after school. Michael Keane never failed to supplement the collection with a personal gift of tuppence, a fortune in those days, since it could buy forty acid drops or thirty-two aniseed balls.

In Church street, where I was born, there lived, next door to us, a wonderful old character whose name was Mick

Broder. By trade he was a harness-maker but his true vocation lay in philosophy. Whenever he had a few pints inside him, it was safe to enter his shop. When he had a sizeable and impressionable audience, he would draw the waxed cord from the needle with which he might be repairing a horse's collar.

'Genkelmen,' Mick would say, 'here is a piece of wax cord.'

He would purse his lips and pucker his brow and a great sigh would escape him. He would look from face to face and hand me the piece of waxed cord.

'Now,' he would say, 'here is the beginning and here is the end. Please hand me back my cord.'

He placed the cord in a tight ball in his fist and opened it out again.

'Now, genkelmen, which is the beginning and which is the end?'

I would point to what I believed to be the end and the beginning. Sadly, Mick would shake his head:

'Wrong as usual, genkelmen. This is the beginning and this is the end.'

Everybody's discernment was put to the test but everybody was wrong. Only Mick knew which was the beginning and which was the end. He died without revealing the secret of his art.

Always as a small boy I had a great longing to go to the mountains, particularly on sunny mornings when the air was fragrant and skies were blue. One could see the mountains at play-time from the back of the school. They stood independent, unchanging and mysterious. They were odd fellows, the mountains – odder than my Uncle Dan, who was as odd as two right boots. When summer hazes tinted their blue outlines they looked unbelievably beautiful and it was hard on a small boy to whom a classroom was prison.

I pestered my parents to let me go and stay with my far-away relatives and eventually they entered into correspondence with them, who, since they had no way of knowing about me, were eager to accept me. My paternal grandmother was a mountainy woman, and that was excuse enough.

At length, as the schoolteachers say, I reached the manly age of eight and the school closed for the summer holidays. When the time came to go to the mountain, I refused, but complaints were arriving at home daily about such heinous offences as robbing orchards and tying pieces of thread to door-knockers. I got a lift from a local Creamery lorry and, with my brown suitcase between my legs, set off into the unknown.

For the next five years I never missed the summer holidays in the Stacks' Mountains. Those were wonderful days and it was there, for the first time, that I met characters who mattered and people who left a real impression. These were lively and vital people, composed of infinite merriment and a little sadness. They lived according to their means and if you didn't like them you could leave them. When they went into town they drank and were misunderstood. Their liveliness and strength was misinterpreted. Rows took place and the age-old hatred of country for town was resurrected. It still exists. It was in the Stacks' Mountains that I discovered that the Holy Ghost was born in Lyreacrompane.

'Some people claim 'twas Glin,' an old man informed me, pointing at a mountain. 'and more says 'tis Clonakilty, but 'tis up there He was born.'

There were several matchmakers in the locality then; six people who had been accused of evil-eye work, and twenty of the most inventive, astonishing and likeable liars on the face of creation.

It was here I learned the great ballad: *'The Road to Athea'*, which contains the classic stanza:

> *'We arrived in Athea at a quarter to one*
> *And up to the clergy we quickly did run;*
> *'Twas there we were married without much delay;*
> *And we broke a spring bed that night in Athea.'*

Money – the little there was in those days – came from the bogs. The turf was black and hard and had a great name in far-away places, like Listowel, Castleisland, and Tralee. There was some employment footing the acres of machine-won turf. The machine was a novelty and people came long distances to see it. I remember there was a German, whose name was Karl Gutthind. He acted as technical adviser to Bord na Mona. When the second World War came he left for Germany. The Russians, I'm sure, must have been surprised at his Lyreacrompane accent and wondered what strange business a Stacksmountain man might have in Stalingrad. He gave me a small flashlight which I swapped a week later for ten Woodbines. Every man has a smile secreted somewhere in his face but I never saw this man smile. Rather it seemed that he was afraid he might and was dead set against such an unprecedented possibility.

There was a Scotsman too, who drove a Baby Ford. He buzzed around the countryside in search of fish. He had a moustache, was completely bald and the outstanding thing I remember about him was that he never gave anybody a drive in his car. It was suggested by some that he was a spy and had bombs in the car but what he was spying on, or what he intended to blow up was a mystery.

To forestall him, if he was a spy, another youngster and I wrote him a note which we left on the bonnet of his car. We threatened him with hanging and signed it 'The Clutching Hand'. He probably thought it was the I. R. A. because we never saw the poor man again.

At night the time was passed by rambling from one house to another, or kicking football in the dry inches along the little river. A next-door neighbour might be a mile or two miles away, but every man, woman and child within a radius of five miles was a neighbour. Wet nights were spent around the fire and there were stories about great men and great deeds. Men were remembered for their prowess with a slean, or a spade or a shovel. Work-horses and ponies were discussed with an affection bordering on love. There was regard for men who bred litters of outstanding bonhams and a man's name might endure whose seed potatoes were incomparable. There were ghost stories, too – tall tales about Jack o' the Lantern and the Puca so that when a fellow went to bed at night he found it hard to sleep and even when the blankets were pulled high over a chap's head, there was no guarantee of safety. One became sorry for fell deeds of days ago, and a jacksnipe bleating in the depths of the bog was surely the drumming hooves of the flame-eyed horses who drew the headless coach through its bitter itinerary.

But in the house where I lived there was an old man, a grand-uncle, who had more insight into the peculiarities of small boys' minds than any man I have ever known. By some uncanny instinct he always knew when a small boy was afraid and he would cough loudly three or four times to let me know I wasn't alone in the world. One could hear the stunted blade of his small knife scraping the black bowl of his pipe, then the scrape of a match, then the cough of satisfaction and a smack of gums which could be heard miles away. He would talk to himself then. He had great sayings.

'By the Lord Harry, but we'll never stick this till morning!' was one.

'Moses was your dacent man!' was another and a third: 'I'm sorry now I ate that Chinaman in Killarney!'

If those didn't work, a fellow could slip in beside him in the bed and no word was spoken till morning. No one was any the wiser either.

Of the children with whom I played in that country of yesterday, the vast majority are gone to England, America, Australia and Canada. They won't hear the vixen barking or the bittern crying wherever they are, and I'll bet they remember the contrary music of that small, wild river and cry sometimes for the shadows of the clouds that galloped like wild ponies across the brown uplands. I've met a few since, holidaying exiles, strangely subdued men with the colour gone from their faces and the old humours departed from their hearts.

After Stacks' Mountains, at the end of my schooldays, I enrolled in the local secondary school – St. Michael's College, Listowel – a branch of the Diocesan Seminary in Killarney. I spent a grand total of six years in St. Michael's and am still remembered there with some pride and affection by the other odd rebels who are occasionally imprisoned there.

I was expelled several times – for smoking, speechmaking, ballad-writing and play-acting. Unfortunately, some of the teachers disliked me because it was politic to do so. The brutality of one particular teacher is something which I will never quite forget. I still have the marks from beatings received on countless occasions, but others suffered as much as I. It may be asked why this sort of brutality was permitted, why parents did not unite in the interests of their children? The answer is, of course, that there was only one secondary school in the town; money was not so plentiful in those days, and most of the parents could not afford boarding-schools. It was a case of enduring it or never learning Greek, Latin or Gaelic – languages incidentally which are very useful when one approaches the foreman of a factory in England!

It was a strange school with a strange charter. There was no football team, no athletics, no competitions of any kind. These things, again, are best forgotten, but one particular thing that remains in my mind.

Long afterwards it is easy to dispel unpleasant memories, because time has done most of the work, but it is extraordinary how long it takes in some instances.

A bad beating is no asset to the self-respect or dignity of an eighteen-year old boy. In some cases it detracts from that sheer fury which we call spirit. In other cases it corrodes, and a boy is defeated. In no case is the ultimate effect advantageous. Misusing an eighteen-year-old is like baiting a three-year old bull. He might not charge there and then but he will explode later on and people find it hard to analyse the reasons.

This incident happened during an elocution class when each boy was expected to quote a few stanzas from some suitable poem. There was no advice beforehand concerning the choice of poem. Presentation was, for the most part, pitiable.

Finally, my turn came to recite, and I made the disastrous mistake of quoting a poem which I had written myself. I had a good ear for poetry and my delivery was a little better than average.

Here's part of the poem. It's called '*Church Street*' –the street where I was born in Listowel:

> '*I love the flags that pave the walk*
> *I love the mud between*
> *The funny figures drawn in chalk*
> *I love to hear the sound*
> *Of drays upon their round*
> *Of horses and their clocklike walk*
> *I love to watch the corner-people gawk*
> *And hear what underlies their idle talk.*

I love to hear the music of the rain
I love to hear the sound
Of yellow waters flushing in the main
I love the breaks between
When little boys begin
To sail their paper galleons in the drain
Grey clouds sail west and silver tips remain
The street, thank God, is bright and clean again.

A golden mellow peace for ever clings
Along the little street
There are so very many lasting things
Beyond the wall of strife
In our beleaguered life
There are so many lovely songs to sing
Of God and His eternal love that rings
Of simple people and of simple things.'

'Who wrote that?' he asked when I had finished.

I did, Father!'

I knew that I had made an impression. I certainly had because there followed the worst beating of all and ejection from the class – which was in no way disturbing, because I had an enjoyable smoke in the lavatory.

What made the beating worse was that there was no explanation for it, but it was this beating which contributed more than anything to my being a writer. That teacher has now departed the scene, and I realise now, too, that he was more to be pitied than blamed. I have since concluded that teaching calls no more for a vocation than shoemaking.

There are many dedicated teachers with rare tact and sensitivity but there are countless others who enter the profession for the comparative security it has to offer and nothing else. Teaching is a gift and should not be looked upon as a cushy and steady type of employment. I also believe that to successfully instruct a class of teenagers, the teacher should be a parent, except in the case of seminaries. A man who has children of his own is not so liekely to mistreat other children. However...

In the end, at the second attempt, I left St. Michael's with a Honours Leaving Certificate.

The previous summer, together with a friend called Murphy, I had worked for three months with a farmer in County Wicklow, but this summer I decided to get a job nearer home. I was fortunate, most fortunate. I got a job as assistant to a fowl-buyer and there followed three of the happiest and most hilarious months of my life.

Some day I will write a play about my fowl-buying period. My associates taught me that porter-drinking was a scientific and ennobling art and that whiskey was a threat to industry, sanity and the sanctity of the family. I became a proficient pint drinker and never regretted it.

I can also say, with some authority, that no man is a proficient drinker of whiskey, that no man has mastered its hallucinatory side-effects and if a man tells you that he has mastered whiskey you can be certain that it is the whiskey that is talking.

CHAPTER

II

I took to fowl-buying with a rare zeal, and Johnny Goggin, a noted exponent, once told me over a pint that I was possessed of all the talents necessary for success in this most engaging profession.

'You know a cock from a hen,' Johnny said, 'and you know horsehair from cow-hair.'

There were unexpected compliments.

'I knows schoolmasters,' said Johnny, 'and with all their smartness, they don't know a hen-egg from a duck-egg!'

All in good time I learned how to kill ducks, geese, chickens, guinea-fowl and turkeys with a little pressure of the fingers and a swift flick of the wrist. I was an art which was difficult to master. The birds left this life without comment and without pain, and I became a member, fully-fledged, of a highly-skilled profession. I was also a passable plucker, even if I do say so myself. I could tell the weight of a tick of feathers to within a few pounds by just glancing at it, and I knew if an old rooster had liver trouble by the look in his eyes. Of all the fowl with which I have been associated, I liked ducks the best. They were the least noisiest when the chips were down and they expired with little fuss which is more than I can say for cockerels.

Work began at eight in the morning and finished any time after six o'clock in the evening. There was no stop for lunch during the day and we depended for sustenance on the generosity of the farmers within the day's prescribed circuit. The poorer the person, the better the prospects if one was fortunate enough to arrive at mealtime. It goes without saying that we saw more mealtimes than meals but our clients were generous to a fault for the most part although one could hardly be expected to pray for a woman who knew a man was hungry but would cut his throat rather than ask him to sit at table, or offer him a solitary spud. It was the smell of bacon and cabbage that unsettled the mental equilibrum. I still sense the haunting aroma of boiling cabbage at odd moments. There were times when I thought bread and butter was the most exotic food in the world. There was one woman, the wife of a farmer whose name I have forgotten, sitting at her table one day in the process of devouring a substantial meal. The action took place near the seaside in the Kerry Head direction. She rose from her meal when I entered with my egg-box and she left the room briefly to fetch her week's collection of eggs. On the plate which taunted me from the table were eleven boiled Brussels sprouts, three small slices of fried streaky bacon and approximately thirty fried chips. In about twenty seconds I had disposed of three Brussels sprouts, one piece of bacon and several chips. It wasn't me... it was the hunger. I had eaten my sandwiches two hours before and I am one who endorses the theory that any given boy can eat any given quantity of food at any given time.

When she returned she looked at the plate and she looked at me. I looked at an old sheepdog who slept near the fire. She said nothing while I counted her eggs. I paid her and still there was no word.

The next day I called she rose from the table, said not a

word, but, looking me between the eyes, took the plate with her to the room where the eggs were.

Some of my poems began to appear at this time in the local and daily papers so that I was a worthy fellow, at least a man of some substance and a chap to be reckoned with when I dressed up to go to the dances in Ballybunion on a Saturday night.

Ballybunion!... if I had a fiver for all the sick heads and unforgettable nights I've had in Ballybunion I could buy a racehorse.

Striped brown suits and bright brown shoes were all the rage at this time, and I had the best in both. Add to these a half-bottle of hair-oil and a carefully constructed lick which tumbled haphazardly over the brow. Add a gleaming white shirt and a vermilion tie and the ultimate result was simply overwhelming. 'Patsy Fagan' and 'Don't Fence me in!' were the hit tunes of the period. I did a mean quickstep, a dreamy waltz, an exuberant if aggressive 'Siege of Ennis' and I could quote Byron, Shelley or Keats when cheek to cheek dancing was involved. My forte, however, was the Tango and I donned my mirror-rehearsed Mexican leer when the occasion demanded it.

Unfortunately, however, I reckoned without the disease of snobbery. During the first Saturday night of my fowl-buying period, the girl with whom I was dancing stopped suddenly and looked at me.

'Aren't you the fellow who buys the feathers?' she said.

'That's right!' I told her cheerfully.

'The cheek of you!' she declared, 'to ask me to dance with you!' and with that she left me standing there. I wouldn't have minded so much but she was a clumsy dancer and was giving me two stone from the weigh-in.

I mentioned it to Johnny Goggin afterwards and his explanation was somewhat circumspect:

'Women is the same as hens,' he said. 'Some boils well and more is hatchers!'

His answer has baffled me to this day.

It was a difficult summer as far as romance was concerned. I found it increasingly difficult to get the local farmers' daughters to dance. When I danced with visiting girls they generally ended by asking me what line of business I was in.

'I'm in the bank,' I said, 'and my uncle is a parish priest.'

That covered a multitude.

The year before I had my first tilt at the stage. My brother Eamonn adapted a sketch from 'Hatter's Castle'. He played Brodie and I played a moneylender who had called at Hatter's Castle to collect an outstanding debt. I had one line of dialogue, which I repeated over and over: 'I want me money, Brodie!' The sketch was part of a show in aid of Jubilee nursing.

There was a full house on that eventful first night. Finally our great moment came and the announcer stood before the footlights with the speech which Eamonn had written for him.

'Ladies and gentlemen,' he began; 'for the first time in any European Theatre, 'Death of a Moneylender', written, produced and acted by Eamonn Keane…'

Not a word about the supporting actor! The curtain went up and we were on. Towards the end I was to repeat the line: 'I want me money, Brodie!' in an irritating manner word, but, looking me between the eyes, took the plate with her to the room where the eggs were.

Some of my poems began to appear at this time in the local and daily papers so that I was a worthy fellow, at least a man of some substance and a chap to be reckoned with when I dressed up to go to the dances in Ballybunion on a Saturday night.

Ballybunion!... if I had a fiver for all the sick heads and unforgettable nights I've had in Ballybunion I could buy a racehorse.

Striped brown suits and bright brown shoes were all the rage at this time, and I had the best in both. Add to these a half-bottle of hair-oil and a carefully constructed lick which tumbled haphazardly over the brow. Add a gleaming white shirt and a vermilion tie and the ultimate result was simply overwhelming. 'Patsy Fagan' and 'Don't Fence me in!' were the hit tunes of the period. I did a mean quickstep, a dreamy waltz, an exuberant if aggressive 'Siege of Ennis' and I could quote Byron, Shelley or Keats when cheek to cheek dancing was involved. My forte, however, was the Tango and I donned my mirror-rehearsed Mexican leer when the occasion demanded it.

Unfortunately, however, I reckoned without the disease of snobbery. During the first Saturday night of my fowl-buying period, the girl with whom I was dancing stopped suddenly and looked at me.

'Aren't you the fellow who buys the feathers?' she said.

'That's right!' I told her cheerfully.

'The cheek of you!' she declared, 'to ask me to dance with you!' and with that she left me standing there. I wouldn't have minded so much but she was a clumsy dancer and was giving me two stone from the weigh-in.

I mentioned it to Johnny Goggin afterwards and his explanation was somewhat circumspect:

'Women is the same as hens,' he said. 'Some boils well and more is hatchers!'

His answer has baffled me to this day.

It was a difficult summer as far as romance was concerned. I found it increasingly difficult to get the local farmers' daughters to dance. When I danced with visiting girls they generally ended by asking me what line of business I was in.

'I'm in the bank,' I said, 'and my uncle is a parish priest.'

That covered a multitude.

The year before I had my first tilt at the stage. My brother Eamonn adapted a sketch from 'Hatter's Castle'. He played Brodie and I played a moneylender who had called at Hatter's Castle to collect an outstanding debt. I had one line of dialogue, which I repeated over and over: 'I want me money, Brodie!' The sketch was part of a show in aid of Jubilee nursing.

There was a full house on that eventful first night. Finally our great moment came and the announcer stood before the footlights with the speech which Eamonn had written for him.

'Ladies and gentlemen,' he began; 'for the first time in any European Theatre, 'Death of a Moneylender', written, produced and acted by Eamonn Keane...'

Not a word about the supporting actor! The curtain went up and we were on. Towards the end I was to repeat the line: 'I want me money, Brodie!' in an irritating manner while Eamonn was speaking. The repetetive demand was supposed to goad him into strangling me. I must have been more irritating than was expected of me, because that night was very nearly my last one on earth. Eamonn entered into the true spirit of his part. When I recovered consciousness fifteen minutes later, the Jubilee nurse shook her head: 'Good job I was in the hall!' she said. An unknown voice in the wings said: 'I was convinced he was dead. That was real acting!'

Later that year I founded my own company. We called ourselves the 'Willie Brothers'. We rented the top floor of the Carnegie Library for a matinee and a night performance. There was singing, dancing, a one-act play written by myself entitled 'The Ghost of Sir Patrick Drury'. There was a fortune-teller, 'Madame Stickorski Darski' who, of course, had appeared before the crowned heads of Europe, who had impressed Hitler, been decorated by Joe Stalin, and was, if one could believe the bills, ravishingly beautiful. The man we chose for the part was Tom Broderick who later became a veterinary surgeon. We dressed him up in a frock of the twenties vintage, procured an outsized stuffed bra for him and purloined a glass globular net-float which served a as crystal ball. The women in the audience sent up written queries demanding descriptions of the type of husband they were likely to marry. No name was signed and Madame, who was blindfolded all through, was expected to identify the writer of each note.

Under the small table, which was draped with muslin, was a small boy who was as wide as the proverbial gate. He relayed the identities to Madame Darski who had little difficulty in identifying the girls with boys in whom they were interested. Madame Stickorski Darski was a resounding success.

We had in our company another distinguished artist whose name was Frank Enright – now in Australia and an actor of some consequence 'down under'. Frank was seventeen. We gave him a moustache and with a dun-pigmented face and a black wig introduced him to the audience as Carl Montana de la Coco Francesco, the Spanish operatic tenor, and explained that he was on holiday in Ballybunion. Certain elements in the body of the hall were sceptical at first, but Frank had one great talent – he could ape the antics of opera singers. He didn't have a note nor could he sing but he had a weird yodel-type protracted yell which he utilised to advantage.

I wrote him a song for the occasion. Here are some of the words:

> *De sorro mallacca lumbago siesta sonoro*
> *Tubacco, two dee fiesta delro tapioca*
> *Cantina muego lumbago siesta la venta*
> *Tubacco, tubacco, mallacca Mike Joe Sacramento*

There were several other verses. A number of elderly but gullible women in the audience were moved to tears when he ended. I will give a special prize to anybody who supplies a translation of the above song.

The final curtain came down to prolonged applause. The show was a success. With prices of admission varying from fourpence to one and threepence, the receipts amounted to eighteen pounds. The money was divided proportionately.

There was no night performance! There was money to be spent and lonely girls in need of consolation and we were wise enough to know that impromptu successes, like win trebles, do not recur.

There followed a succession of skittish sketches and one-act plays. These fitted nicely into other concerts when funds were low and money was an urgent necessity.

The summer and all youthful summers ended and I was faced with choosing a career. My brother Eamonn, not long before, packed his traps one morning and quietly disappeared without telling anybody. The next we heard from him was that he was learning to be an actor in, of all places, the Abbey Theatre.

Consequently, much consultation took place and many novenas were said for my sake.

CHAPTER

III

I have no objection to prayers and novenas, as long as they are said by people who have a direct interest in my life's plan. I seem to attract a good deal of unnecessary prayer.

One night, after the premiere of my play, '*The Highest House on the Mountain,*' in the 1960 Theatre Festival, a lanky, wicked-looking lady with an umbrella, raised it over the heads of the producer, Barry Cassin, and myself as we were leaving the theatre, and told us she was going to pray for us. The play was essentially a Christian one, with a Christian message. It was well received by all the Irish and English papers and the Maynooth magazine, '*The Furrow,*' was favourable. I have often asked myself why this woman should want to pray for me when she might be neglecting herself. The number of anonymous letters I receive from such signatories as 'Good Catholic', 'Catholic Mother' and so on are never read. I examine the end of each epistle I receive and, if no name is provided, I straightaway burn the letter. Sometimes holy pictures are enclosed and this, to my mind, is downright blackguardism since I would not like to burn holy pictures.

After an unpleasant sojourn at St. Michael's, I was apprenticed to a chemist in Listowel. My boss was the kindest of men, and we liked each other – which is the most important of all. I never showed any interest in qualifying, which was a disappointment to him and to my parents. After five years of bottle-shaking, powder-mixing, tablet-counting and wart-curing, I saw the futility of my existence staring me in the face like a bottomless black pit.

I wrote little during this period. I played a good deal of Gaelic football and a little Rugby and enjoyed myself at both. I competed at sports-meetings and was a nifty hundred-yards man, a useful long-jumper and not too easily beaten in the two-twenty. One evening I told my boss that I wanted to be a writer and that I was thinking of going to England.

'It's as easy to write here as there!' he said; but, of course, I couldn't be expected to know that at the time.

Around this time, too, in Listowel, Stan Kennelly and I started a newspaper. We called it 'The Listowel Leader.' It was a stencil job. The first and only edition consisted of 960 copies, which were bought overnight out of sheer curiosity. It was a twelve-page paper. We sold six pages of advertisements. The price was threepence and we made a profit – not a large profit but enough to make the work we put into it worthwhile. Our circulation managers were two local girls, Kats Lynch and Marie Keane-Stack, who later played opposite Mac Liammoir in the Gate Theatre in L.A.G. Strong's play 'The Director'.

I also played opposite Mac Liammoir but under different circumstances. It was in the Spring of 1961 in Queen's University, Belfast, when we debated the over-debated Irish Theatre before several hundred students.

There was no second edition of 'The Listowel Leader' for the good reason that we incurred the wrath of a few local councillors. In the editorial a savage attack was made on those whom we believed were responsible for the deplorable condition of the town park. The line which gave offence was this: '*You can send a message to a maiden aunt in New Jersey in a fraction of a second, but it can take you years to send a plain fact through a quarter-inch of official skull!*' They put the fear of God into us and plans for expansion, luckily for us, ended prematurely.

Perhaps the most enjoyable episode of those years was the invention of a character called Tom Doodle. The idea originated in Curly's. Curly's is a pub in Listowel where we would occasionally foregather to do a little chanting and imbibing. We overheard a man singing a song:

> '*Tom Doodle don't know that his father is dead;*
> *And his father don't know that Tom Doodle is dead…*'

We found it intriguing. This was 1951. The time was a month before the General Election. We were sick of the vicious exchanges overheard in pubs and at street-corners and felt that a resurrected Tom Doodle was just the man to take the sting out of local politics.

First of all, we had to find him, however. After a judicious and exhausting search we discovered an experienced actor who would oblige us free of charge. We then found a local man, of astonishing innocence, who was willing to act as Tom Doodle's representative in the area. His name was Michael but it was decided that Michael Gulliver sounded more attractive. We called ourselves the Independent Coulogeous Party. We drew up a Four-Point Plan:

1 To Plough the Rocks of Bawn;

counting and wart-curing, I saw the futility of my existence staring me in the face like a bottomless black pit.

I wrote little during this period. I played a good deal of Gaelic football and a little Rugby and enjoyed myself at both. I competed at sports-meetings and was a nifty hundred-yards man, a useful long-jumper and not too easily beaten in the two-twenty. One evening I told my boss that I wanted to be a writer and that I was thinking of going to England.

'It's as easy to write here as there!' he said; but, of course, I couldn't be expected to know that at the time.

Around this time, too, in Listowel, Stan Kennelly and I started a newspaper. We called it 'The Listowel Leader.' It was a stencil job. The first and only edition consisted of 960 copies, which were bought overnight out of sheer curiosity. It was a twelve-page paper. We sold six pages of advertisements. The price was threepence and we made a profit – not a large profit but enough to make the work we put into it worthwhile. Our circulation managers were two local girls, Kats Lynch and Marie Keane-Stack, who later played opposite Mac Liammoir in the Gate Theatre in L.A.G. Strong's play 'The Director'.

I also played opposite Mac Liammoir but under different circumstances. It was in the Spring of 1961 in Queen's University, Belfast, when we debated the over-debated Irish Theatre before several hundred students.

There was no second edition of 'The Listowel Leader' for the good reason that we incurred the wrath of a few local councillors. In the editorial a savage attack was made on those whom we believed were responsible for the deplorable condition of the town park. The line which gave offence was this: '*You can send a message to a maiden aunt in New Jersey in a fraction of a second, but it can take you years to send a plain fact through a quarter-inch of official skull!*' They put the fear of God into us and plans for expansion, luckily for us, ended prematurely.

Perhaps the most enjoyable episode of those years was the invention of a character called Tom Doodle. The idea originated in Curly's. Curly's is a pub in Listowel where we would occasionally foregather to do a little chanting and imbibing. We overheard a man singing a song:

> '*Tom Doodle don't know that his father is dead;*
> *And his father don't know that Tom Doodle is dead...*'

We found it intriguing. This was 1951. The time was a month before the General Election. We were sick of the vicious exchanges overheard in pubs and at street-corners and felt that a resurrected Tom Doodle was just the man to take the sting out of local politics.

First of all, we had to find him, however. After a judicious and exhausting search we discovered an experienced actor who would oblige us free of charge. We then found a local man, of astonishing innocence, who was willing to act as Tom Doodle's representative in the area. His name was Michael but it was decided that Michael Gulliver sounded more attractive. We called ourselves the Independent Coulogeous Party. We drew up a Four-Point Plan:

1 To Plough the Rocks of Bawn;

2 Expansion of the periwinkle industry;
3 Free treatment for 'sick heads';
4 Erection of a factory for shaving the hair from gooseberries.

We printed these on large placards and pinned them to the telegraph and light-poles all over the town and country. We also had bills printed announcing the arrival of Tom Doodle. After Mass on Sundays and at football matches we handed around handbills which counselled the electorate to '*Use your noodle; vote for Doodle*,' and '*Give the whole caboodle to Doodle.*'

Our campaign annoyed some people, but the majority received us well. At last the day of Doodle's promised arrival came. Several thousand people crowded the town from an early hour that evening. Two local bands, who had been at variance for years, joined forces and were waiting at the railway station for the great man's arrival. Earlier Michael Gulliver, two others and I collected the gentleman who was to play the part and drove to Kilmorna railway station, a few miles outside Listowel. We dressed the actor in swallow-tail coat, tall hat and spats. We gave him a wig and a flowing beard. At the last second, three of us – Doodle and his two bodyguards – boarded the train at Kilmorna.

We did not have time to purchase tickets, but the conductor, realising he was in the presence of a dignitary, ushered us into a first-class carriage.

We were, as we neared Listowel, naturally a little apprehensive, but George Finucane, my fellow bodyguard – God rest him! – had brought along a half-pint of brandy in anticipation of last-minute butterflies. In a moment the bottle was drained, and the train drew to a stop at our native town.

A crowd of several hundred waited and a guard of honour three rows deep stretched for fifty yards outside the entrance to the station. Tom Murphy, our local butcher and a member of the Independent Coulogeous Party, welcomed Tom Doodle, who immediately pinned medals on Murphy and other members of the Executive. He also kissed them on both cheeks and conferred on us, his bodyguards, the honour of M.I.D. (Most Insignificant Order of Doodle).

The night before, the Taoiseach of the time had conducted a rally in Listowel. Doodle drew a crowd which was more than twice as large. The night was a triumph for the Independent Coulogeous Party. Tom Doodle was whisked away, despite the clamour of thousands, and the perseverance of souvenir-hunters. To this day nobody knows his identity but the memory of him is as fresh as ever and his visit is commemorated on the 31st of January of every year since his first appearance. It is a strange sight to see thirty grown men from all walks of life pounding around the streets of Listowel singing the Doodle Anthem:

> *'Our song is sung for Doodle, Tom;*
> *He made us free;*
> *He is no gom, our Doodle, Tom,*
> *The champion of love and liberty...'*

The parade ends in Market street where the party enter cars and go to Ballybunion for a specially-prepared dinner after which two firkins of stout are tapped and merriment endures till morning. No woman is permitted to attend or take any part in the long ceremony. The party also marches through Ballybunion, down the Main street and up Doon Road with the Atlantic stretching to infinity beneath. Each man wears a sash and a dickie-bow. Two musicians march in the van – one playing a fife: the other a battle-drum. Outside the dining-hall the dinner-song is chanted:

> *'Let porter fresh from laughing barrels*
> *Abolish life's unending quarrels;*
> *And pray no man endure the colic*
> *That doth attend Tom Doodle's frolic…'*

It was in September, 1951, that I first met Mary, the girl I eventually married, the mother of my sons, and one who must be blamed even more than I for the writings I have produced.

It was firmly in my head for some time to emigrate to America, and it was probably the hopelessness of my position with regard to marriage that was most responsible for my leaving Ireland.

So, on the 6th of January, 1952, I set out to make my fortune.

I chose England. It was nearer for one thing, and many of my friends were already settled down there. I decided to apply beforehand to Boots Chemists for a position. It was better, my father said, to have something waiting over – 'something that will keep the bite in your mouth, anyway!' he said. I said goodbye to Mary. It was a tearful one, but I would be home in the summertime for a holiday, a long wait between dates, however.

In Dublin I met Eamonn. He was with Radio Eireann then. It was to be some time before he had his disastrous clash with the Minister for Posts and Telegraphs. We celebrated the beginning of my exile in true style. We started at three o'clock in the Tower Bar at the corner of Henry Street and O'Connell Street and I made the eight o'clock boat with only minutes to spare.

I was more than slightly intoxicated but not even that could dispel the gloom which I felt at leaving home for the first time. I remember, as I walked up the gangplank, I heard Eamonn shouting after me. 'Write!' he yelled. 'Write something every day... Write... Write...' His voice tailed off. There were hundreds of other good-byes.

When I boarded the train at Listowel that morning it seemed as if everyone was leaving. It was the same at every railway station along the way. Dun Laoghaire, for the first time, was a heartbreaking experience – the goodbyes to husbands going back after Christmas, chubby-faced boys and girls leaving home for the first time, bewilderment written all over them, hard-faced old-stagers who never let on but who felt it the worst of all because they knew only too well what lay before them.

It was a cold night, with high seas as they say. Conditions were shocking – that is for second-class passengers, or, if you like, the steerage-type exile, which breed constituted the great majority of my fellow-travellers.

In my hip-pocket I had a naggin of Irish whiskey. It was a poor consolation, a parting gift from Eamonn whose last words were still ringing in my ears. Maybe if I stuck to writing it might eventually get me back to Ireland.

I joined forces with a pale-faced, red-haired woman whose name was Nora. She was the mother of five children and she was trying to look after the five on that draughty deck. She was on her way to join her husband in London. After two years of separation, neither could tolerate it. He was lucky to find a two-roomed flat at four pounds a week in the suburbs of London.

Years later, in 1960, when my first play '*SIVE*' was presented, unsuccessfully, at the Lyric Theatre in Hammersmith, Nora arrived with her husband and eldest daughter. She had not thought of me, or heard of me, since the night of the crossing, but saw my photograph in an English daily paper and booked for the play at the last minute. She had forgotten when we first met to ask me what line of business I was in. If I was being hanged at Hammersmith she would have been there with a placard.

All around us as we left Dun Laoghaire, there was drunkenness. The younger men were drunk – not violently so but tragically so, as I was, to forget the dreadful loneliness of having to leave home. Underneath it all was the heartbreaking, frightful anguish of separation. It would be a waste of time for me to launch into a description of what went on. A person has to be part of it to feel it. The whole scene reminded me of the early Christian martyrs going out to face the terrors of the arena. Laugh if you like, but there was an unbelievable spirit of fraternity, a kind of brotherhood, a communal feeling of tragedy which embraced us all.

It is no laughing matter to those who took part in the pilgrimage.

Everybody was helping somebody else. A few rough diamonds came to the assistance of Nora and took charge of the five children. They looked after their every want till morning. One man of about fifty, a time-scarred bucknavvy, insisted on changing a nappy. It was just a formality. He wasn't embarrassed and nobody took any notice. It would have been a real tragedy if somebody did. Of all the things I've ever felt or seen, nothing ever so moved or affected me as the sight of these men and women being torn away from home. If you want to laugh, now is your chance. Laugh loud and high and you'll be heard by some lonely old couple whose loved ones are lost forever.

Recently in Dun Laoghaire, in hotels and loungebars where I have been accorded some attention by the proprietors and others of consequence from the neighbourhood, I was tempted to elaborate on the theme of departure from the pier when I was asked if I liked Dun Laoghaire or if it was my first visit.

It wasn't!

They wouldn't have felt or understood the anguish of perpetual departure. For them Dun Laoghaire was a soft bed, good fires and excellent reception from cross-channel telly. For us, as it was then, it was the brink of hell and don't think I use the word hell lightly! If there is an artist in this country – a real artist who wants to capture the truth for eternity on his canvases – my advice to him is to go to the North Wall, to Dun Laoghaire, to Rosslare or to Cork. Watch the faces, and, unless you're a heartless inhuman moron, you'll feel something and your conscience will begin to bother you. I have been accused on several occasions of highlighting the problem of emigration and of evading the issue of a solution. The solution is – don't go! Stay at home. We are your people and this is your country.

We – the ones at home – are responsible for you.

A country is like a parent. It must provide for its children, so stay at home, and when the urge which is part of the heritage of the Irish race takes hold of you, plant your feet firmly on your own soil and don't go. I have heard England referred to as the land of cups of cha, the land of jellied eels, etc. All this is most derogatory. At least the English are a race who look after their own. They conquered the world to provide for younger sons.

It is all right if you're English, or that way inclined, but to me, and to millions of others, it means banishment.

Don't go! Don't panic! This is our country. That's all you have to remember.

Another thing the uninitiated second-class exile will long remember is the contempt of elusive stewards and channel officers for our type of cargo. It is never expressed in words – they wouldn't dare (we'd break their necks if they did!) – but it is written over their faces: contempt, scorn and disinterestedness. The tourist is fawned over and spoiled, but they can't wait to deposit the departing Paddy on the other side.

How different it is all coming back for the annual holiday: the melodeons and fiddles and the sing-songs, the exuberant boys and the friendly girls, the attentiveness of the grasping stewards and the cheerful quips flung at the generous Paddies who cannot spend it quickly enough. Back again then when the short holiday is over.

The pangs of leaving grow worse with every passage and, as time passes, there are no more homecomings. For a good percentage of the Irish race there is no returning to 'die at home at last'.

It follows a fixed pattern. The young will keep coming back each year until the parents die.

On the deck that night, despite the cold and the heartbreak, there was singing.

The singing was drunken singing, but it was not without dignity. There were songs in Gaelic, and many groups conversed entirely in Gaelic which made them suspect immediately from the stewards' point of view. There were girls in groups ranging in ages from fifteen to eighteen. They were no older than the boys. There were women with babies and women with large families, like my newly-found friend, Nora. There were a few older women, going over to daughters who were expecting babies: others to daughters whose husbands had deserted them: and still others in search of sons who had not written home for several years and of whom there was no trace despite enquiries by police and clergy.

There was eagerness written on the younger faces. This would be their first time. Always the first time, despite the loneliness, there is an air of adventure. Not so the second and third times and the times after that.

One girl of sixteen caught my attention. She was pretty and healthy with an innocent childish face. She was an attractive child. In ten years – unless she was lucky – she would be trying to rear her two or three or more children in a single room, or, at best, a room and kitchen. She would have no way of knowing this. She wasn't educated for it.

All the songs that were being sung were songs of overwhelming sadness. '*All our wars are merry, and all our songs are sad,*' wrote Chesterton. A group of five men, who had a case of beer between them, were singing the songs of the Long-Distance Man and the Buck-Navvy – songs like the songs that Patrick McGill gave to Moleskin Joe:

> ''*Twas in the pub we drank the sub;*
> *We drank it with good cheer…*'

There was another song, which I have forgotten – but it might run like this:

Come all you true-born Irishmen, and listen to my song.
I am a bold buck-navvy and I don't know right from wrong.
Of late I was transported, boys, from Erin's holy shore;
My case is sad, my crime is bad, for I was born poor.

And if you're born poor, my boys, that is a woeful state;
The judge will sit upon your crime and this he will relate:
'I find the prisoner guilty and the law I must lay down:
Let this man be transported straightaway to Camden Town.'

Then take him down to Cricklewood and lock him in the pub:
And call the Limey guv'nor and propose him for the sub;
Yes, take him down to Cricklewood, to mortar bricks and lime

And let him rot in Cricklewood until he serves his time.

Between each verse, there would be the refrain:

> *'Oh, Cricklewood, Oh, Cricklewood,*
> *You stole my youth away;*
> *For I was young and innocent,*
> *And you were old and gray.'*

And Cricklewood is old and gray, and so is Camden Town, and so is Lime Street Station in Liverpool, and so is Northampton – and it was to the town of Northampton that I was bound.

After several hours we disembarked at Holyhead, dirty and shapeless at half-past one in the morning.

We boarded an endless train and sped through the dark. We could not know that we were fleeting past historic landmarks and through towns like Bangor, Conway, Chester, and Stafford. If somebody had pointed out these facts to us it would have been interesting to hear our comments.

At Rugby I said goodbye to Nora and her family. They were on their way to London. There was no singing now in any of the compartments. The fatigue had taken the gimp out of the singers and reality was very close.

I was the only passenger to alight at Rugby. The junction was utterly deserted and if there is a murderer reading this I recommend Rugby Junction at four-thirty on a January morning. There will be no witnesses and the echoing cries of the victim will add to the effects.

A small man with a peaked cap and a long oil-can passed, bearing a lantern.

'I beg your pardon,' I said, 'but could you tell me what time the next train leaves for Northampton?'

"S gone, mate!' he replied.

'Gone?'

"S just gone, mate!'

'When is the next one?'

'Next one's at six-thirty. Got any cigs, mate?'

I gave him a cigarette and he continued down the line. I watched his light for a long while and was lonesome when it disappeared around a bend in the railway. I sat in the waiting-room but the cold was intense. The toilets had the haunting hollowness of a morgue. It seemed a sacrilege to use them for their normal purposes, but nature is not so easily baulked.

Until the Northampton train arrived at six o'clock I saw no sign of life – not even a cat. Murphy – a pal of my schooldays – met me in the morning when the train arrived at Northampton. His first question reminded me of Jim Hawkins and Ben Gunn.

'Did you bring any Aftons?'

I had a carton. He took my bag and we walked. There were no buses running so early. We walked through miles of streets.

'This bag has me killed,' Murphy said. 'What's in it?'

'There's a bottle of whiskey,' I said. 'It's a gift from me to you.'

Without a word, he placed the bag on a convenient windowsill and we located the whiskey.

'Here's to Mother Ireland!' he toasted.

'The same here!' I said, taking the bottle.

He put the bottle in his overcoat pocket and it was empty by the time we reached our destination. Murphy knocked at the door but there was no reply. It was a goodlooking well-kept house on the outside and the curtains were attractive – always a good sign of a house. Murphy knocked again and finally a small fat woman of middle-age with a cigarette in her mouth and a tam on her head, opened the door.

'I'm not 'aving 'im!' she said.

'Why not?' Murphy demanded.

'I'm not 'avin' Paddies!' She was adamant.

'He's not a Paddy,' Murphy said. 'He's a Jock the same as myself.'

'Awright,' she asked quickly, 'which part you from?'

'Glasgie!' I lied, without batting an eyelid.

Finally, she said: 'You'd better come in, then.'

My arrival brought her complement of lodgers to ten, five to a room. There were two Poles. We called them Joe No. One and Joe No. Two. Nobody ever learned what their real names were. They were Catholics – non-practising ones, but more about that later. There were four of us from the same town and the same school – Murphy, Grogan, Pat Stack and myself.

The landlord's name was 'Enery Atkinson. His wife's name was Beryl. Neither practised religion of any kind but from a moral viewpoint they were a model couple, deeply attached to each other. The lodgings, for all their cramp-iness, were clean and the food was excellent. We had a sitting-room of our own where we could sit and talk when funds were low.

There were two North of Ireland men – Frank and

Jimmy – and two Welsh labourers who always regarded us with the deepest suspicion. They resented us – suspected we were Irish, but were afraid to say so.

In the hallway, as one entered from the street, there was a most engaging and unusual notice pinned to the wall. It was written in large, readable longhand and it was obvious that a good deal of time and thought had gone into its composition. It ran something like this:

'NOTICE TO GUESTS'

'Guests will not use chamber pots, bed pans, urinals or commodes in bedrooms. Guests will not keep cage-birds, dogs or pets of any kind. Guests will not entertain female visitors. Guests will not spit while indoors. Guests will not bring alcoholic drinks into bedrooms. Guests will flush toilets immediately after use.'

I once translated it into pidgin English for Joe the Pole No. Two. He had always believed it was a house blessing, and he took a dim view of the Atkinsons thereafter.

When Beryl finally discovered we were Irish she promptly gave us our notice. She wouldn't have found out at all but a doorman in a downtown Ballroom had been kicked to death by a number of men who were allegedly Paddies the first Saturday night after my arrival, and there was intense police activity for a few days. Two detectives called to our digs while we were out and left when they discovered that we were at work on the night in question. When we arrived from work Joe the Pole No. One told us what had transpired.

Our dinner was on the table as always after we had changed but Beryl was unusually reserved and there was none of the customary banter. Towards the end of the meal she made the following announcement:

'You told me you was Jocks when you was downright Paddies all along. I'm not 'avin' no Paddies in this 'ouse. It says so on me window.'

This was true enough. Most of the windows along the street had notices to the same effect: *'No negroes, no Irish,'* with *'This means you, Paddy!'* in italics underneath.

We packed, paid her and departed. We were halfway down the street when she called us back. When we returned she had gone upstairs but 'Enery was waiting in the hallway.

'You chaps is all right,' he said. 'No two people is alike, I reckon.'

He told us afterwards that Beryl cried when we left. Shortly after that she gave notice to the two Poles. Her reasons may seem strange when one considers that she was an utter Atheist. One Sunday morning Joe No. One and Joe No. Two did not get out of bed till lunchtime. She told them that if they missed Mass again she would let them go. The next Sunday morning when they failed to come downstairs in time she ordered them out and even when they made a contrite return a few days afterwards and told her that they had reformed, she refused to take them in. We were sorry to see them go. They were quiet inoffensive men who were perpetually bewildered by their surroundings. The English tolerated them, but only barely. They were foreigners and most of the time they were made to feel it. We got on well with them, perhaps because we understood them better. Like us, they were exiles, but while we had some chance of returning, there was no hope whatsoever that they would see Poland again. They were frequently depressed and often sullen. A man without a country is as confused as a dog without a tail. He knows he has lost something but he can't put his finger on it. He also knows that no other tail will replace the one he has lost. In other words he doesn't belong to a particular denomination any more.

Mrs. Atkinson, or Beryl, was a scrupulously honest woman. She was no exception as far as most English landladies went. 'Enery, as we called him, was fair and decent. I remember one night during a particularly bad thunderstorm, we were early in bed in readiness for a morning shift in a factory. We were talking about women, home and money – in that order. A sudden lightning flash lighted the room and a deafening clap of thunder followed.

'Holy Water,' someone whispered.

'I'll go downstairs,' Murphy said, 'if someone will come with me.'

We went downstairs together. 'Enery was in the kitchen filling in his Pool coupons and Beryl was knitting by the fire.

'Wot's up?' 'Enery asked.

'Any sup o' Holy Water in the house?' Murphy asked.

''Oly what?' 'Enery said, looking mystified at Beryl.

'Holy Water!' Murphy repeated.

'I've 'eard of tonic water, Vichy water and sulphur water,' 'Enery said, 'but I've never 'eard of 'oly water!'

We explained in detail to 'Enery what Holy Water was and how it was used. At first he thought we were pulling his leg but in the end he believed us. Beryl was mystified but never said a word. The following evening when we came in from work there was an elaborate Holy Water font attached to the wall in the hallway. More important, it was full.

'That's all right,' Grogan said, 'but what kind of water is in it?'

Murphy dipped his finger in, and tasted it first.

'It tastes like holy water,' he said and he blessed himself. 'I was an altar-boy once,' he explained. 'I'd know the taste of holy water anywhere.'

Afterwards the holy water font was never empty. The Atkinsons used it most of all. Before going on journeys, no matter how short, they sprinkled themselves liberally. Beryl once went to Hull to visit a sister-in-law. An important item of her luggage was a half-pint bottle of Holy Water.

Both 'Enery and Beryl disliked the Irish and not without reason. When they first set up a boarding establishment during the Second World War, they kept a number of Irish tradesmen and labourers. On one occasion their house was wrecked. Another time 'Enery was badly beaten. Fights were commonplace and no boarder, especially if he were English, was safe when the wild Irish were on the rampage.

I remember the story told about a black man who stayed in the same digs as a number of Irishmen in London. On St. Patrick's night they returned home from what is loosely called a social. They roused the other boarders and sent them scurrying into the streets. When they came to the black man's room, he threw his hands heavenwards and screamed: 'Me Culchie, too! Me Culchie, too!'

It is hard to know when, exactly, the Irish got a bad name

in England. There is a good side, too, and the prestige of Irish nurses is without comparison. In fact, the behaviour of seventy-five per cent of Irish emigrants is unquestionably exemplary but the other twenty-five per cent nullifies the advantage. I knew two English pubs in Northampton where no soldiers in British uniform dare enter. This might strike a sympathetic note with certain elements, such as England-haters and extremists, but it does little for our stock abroad. The attitude of the average Englishman towards the Irish is a friendly one. He resents the Welshman and tolerates the Scot but he is prepared to enjoy the Irishman and will always meet him half-way. On the other hand, the infamous 'Black Maria' would no longer be in use in Manchester, Liverpool or London but for the Irish brawls on Saturday nights. All very painful, the patriot will say – but the bitter truth nevertheless.

Why is it, one will ask, that the Irish in present-day America are held in such high esteem as compared with their kinsmen in Britain. The answer is obvious. There is no sort of aptitude test for British-bound emigrants. They need not be claimed by relatives and a prison record is no ban to entry. Does this mean, then, that the cream of our youth go to America and the scruff to England? No – it does not, because most of the Irish in England are highly regarded, but while Irish Justices and Judges persist in sending rowdies and criminals back to England for offences committed in Ireland, Irish prestige abroad is always in danger of deflation. The undesired Irish elements usually hunt in packs. They court and invite trouble and can always be trusted to make their own fights. Doormen, barmen, policemen and chuckers-out are the chief victims, and indeed anybody whose face they might happen to dislike or anybody who is foolish enough to look sideways at them.

The best advice that can be offered to the young Irish emigrant is this. Always stay with a relation, or somebody you know well, for a start. Avoid all Irishmen until you are in a position to assimilate character-traits from experience. Avoid Irish pubs and notorious Irish dance-halls as you would a plague. Contact the secretary, or priest, in charge of the local Irish club and you won't go far wrong.

But this should not be the job of the teenage emigrant. It is the duty of parents to make contacts and enquiries beforehand. Parents do not do this, however, and that is why so many of our boys and girls take the wrong road. I am in no position to judge anybody but I hope God will be very hard on parents who ship bewildered little boys and girls off to England when they have no idea of the conditions there. Yet, no matter what provision is made, England is no place for the under-schooled unattached boy or girl of eithteen to twenty-one. If England is to be the lot of these impressionable adolescents, it should be the lot of their heartless fathers and mothers too.

Three days after I arrived in England I got a job in a chemist's shop at £7.17.6 per week. It was a small branchshop which catered almost exclusively for national health customers and a nice bunch of greedy pill-gobbling bottle-sucking characters they were. If it was free they tried it! My boss was a small baldheaded snob named Sid. There was also a girl apprentice named Gloria who was terrified of him. Like most small men, he made a lot of noise when he walked. He loathed the Irish for uncited reasons. He insisted on calling me Paddy but he stopped when I started to call him Paddy, too. Once, in a leering fashion, he asked me what the 'B.' in my name stood for.

'Basketball!' I told him.

On another occasion, during a heated argument, I pointed out to him that Wellington was a Dublin man and that Kitchener was a Listowel man. He accepted Wellington but bet me a pound that Kitchener was as English as himself. He learned in the local library that night that Kitchener was indeed born a few miles from Listowel but refused to hand over the pound on the grounds that the Irish-hating Lord General was not born in the town itself.

My position became intolerable and I jacked it up without regret.

It was about this time that Murphy decided to offer himself to the Royal Navy and he persuaded me into going along with him.

'The navy's the place for young chaps like you,' 'Enery said.

The night before we departed a small party of close friends made its way home from the 'Black Boy', a downtown watering place.

In the morning, we hitch-hiked to Portsmouth and arrived there by car, truck and van, at 12.30 that night. Early the day after we rose, dressed and paid our bill, three-and-sixpence per head for bed only, and made our wearisome way to the recruiting office.

A cheerful petty officer greeted us and gave us forms to fill in. We managed without difficulty.

'What's this?' he said.

'What's what?' said we.

'This 'ere, cock,' he said, pointing to our nationalities.

'What's wrong with it?' Murphy demanded.

'Everything's wrong with it,' the sailor explained. 'In the first place, you're British subjects and should 'ave said so 'ere!' He pointed a pink finger at my error.

'We're not British subjects,' I reminded him.

'Oh, yes, you are!' he said. 'Your parents was British subjects, therefore you're British subjects.'

'Say that again!' Murphy said.

'Now, look 'ere!' he said; 'We get chaps like you regular. Do you want to joint the navy or don't you?'

'We're Irishmen!' Murphy said.

An hour later we counted our money in a cafe. The time was twelve fifteen. The Royal Navy suffered a terrible defeat on that day, even if it doesn't know about it. It lost a probable Drake and a possible Nelson.

We had four shillings and a penny between us. It took us a day and a half to get back to Northampton.

We arrived back, starving and out of work. We got lodgings at another end of the town with a lady whose identity I prefer not to disclose. There were several other boarders. We slept three to a room which would have been tolerable if there was any degree of cleanliness. Murphy got a job driving a breadvan and I signed on with the Corporation as a street-cleaner or scavenger. The work was light enough but we were on the streets at all hours of the morning.

You'd be amazed at some of the things that happen when

the world is supposed to be in bed and you wouldn't believe the number of broken milk-bottles and empty cigaretteboxes which reappear every morning.

The Irish nurses on their way to the general hospital always stopped to talk to us and I made many lasting friends.

The street-cleaner occupies a very low rung in the social ladder as I discovered after a week. We were concluding our operations one bright morning when I beheld a professional man whom I had known in Ireland strolling along the street as if he were returning from an extremely successful late-night party. He sobered up quickly enough when I saluted him, looked at me panic-stricken, recognized me and turned his head away. Hurriedly he disappeared around the nearest available corner. I felt sorry for this unfortunate man and still do. There are thousands like him who never can make up their mind whether they should salute people or not. They cannot even be quite sure about their own sorry grades in the local social register. What a horrible way to have to live a life. God pity their penny-halfpenny presumption and grant them respite from the uncertainty of their self- imposed afflictions because these are the unlucky ones who have failed to adapt themselves to improved circumstances.

I endured the Corporation for two months during which time I wrote a short novel in the Patrick McGill style. It was returned to me by no fewer than eight publishers.

The digs during this time were downright disgraceful, the beds and bedclothes filthy but the landlady, God bless her, was the filthiest of all. The food was unbelievable. It was nearly always stew and when it wasn't stew it was 'steak and kidney pud' bought at the rate of two-and-ninepence a tin at a shop in the city centre. There was a joint on Sundays but there was never enough to go round and what did go around was sloppy and inedible. I was sick for a few weeks during this period and was badly run down but you don't go to bed when there's no taste of food or drink, when the landlady resents it and tells you to go to hospital.

We left these digs and tried another, recommended by a Corporation colleague. This woman had never kept boarders before and I fervently hope that she never will again. It was sausage and mash day in, day out. The mash was bad enough but no self-respecting dog would have a second go at the sausages. The beds were clean, however, and the room was spotless but the absence of meat was unbearable, and we tried another lodgings. There were a few Irishmen already staying there but after witnessing two drunken rows on successive Saturday nights we left in a hurry. We rented a room and took turns at the cooking and for the first time we had meat. None of us could cook, unfortunately, and we were continually on the look-out for good digs.

One Sunday night in the 'Black Boy' we caught sight of 'Enery and Beryl Atkinson again. They were seated in an small lounge off the bar. We ordered drinks and had them sent in. 'Enery quickly appeared to thank his unknown benefactors and when he saw who it was he stopped dead in his tracks.

'Where's your uniforms?' was the first thing he said.

Beryl, when she saw who it was, quickly joined him. Without elaboration, we unfolded the history of our misfortunes. Beryl wept as usual and even 'Enery was moved. We drank copiously and were forced to order a taxi to take the four of us home. But we slept that night under the benign wing of Beryl Atkinson and 'Enery promised to see if he could get us positions with the firm where he was employed.

It was the first comfortable night's sleep we had in two months and the first night we dipped our fingers in holy water before going to bed.

Our fellow-boarders were delighted to see us and they regaled us with a detailed account of the savoury meals. Beryl had cooked for them since we left to join the navy, It was strange to see fellows kneeling by their beds agains saying their prayers,

The following afternoon, when 'Enery returned from work, he had good news.

CHAPTER

IV

'Enery was a fitter, a good one.

He was employed by an Anglo-American steel company, British Timken. They manufactured roller bearings and had a monopoly in England. On his recommendation we were taken on.

My first week was spent brushing the floors free of oil and sand. I was issued with wooden clogs by the firm and when my first week was completed I was appointed as assistant to a furnace operator. I was accepted into the Union and for the first time since my arrival in England I was invited to join a Labour Club.

Now, in case you get the wrong impression, there are good Labour Clubs. The one I was invited to join, however, was a Communist one. One is not expected to know this at first but I quickly saw through the unassuming specially-trained operator who approached me. He was as Irish as I was. He had passed his Leaving Certificate. We smoked and talked during the teabreak for a few days. We had a good deal in common, the same grievances and much the same background. He was a real nice fellow and you couldn't help but appreciate his sincerity. I thought that if I gave him enough rope he would hang himself but he was far too polished and well-instructed for that. In the end, in as mild a tone as possible. I asked him if he was a Communist. He made no denial and boasted that he had plenty friends in the factory. As I discovered later, he had about twenty – all dyed-in-the-wool redcoats, as the union members called them. About half the twenty were Irish. They were all semi-educated and self-educated. There was not one of what, for my purpose, I will call the peasant class. The British and Irish Communist parties, like the Russian, are fairly exclusive – even snobbish.

In this factory there were approximately 200 Irish workers. Five per cent were positively communistic – a startling figure.

Recently an Irish priest pointed out that there were seven hundred communists in Ireland. I disagree with him. I would say that there are 1,500 and I would say that there is at least the same number of Irish communists in England. About thirty per cent are female.

The Irish worker in England is the best target for the Communist canvasser.

Wherever you find resentment, irreverence, dissatisfaction and loneliness inhabiting the same human spirit, you will find a prospective candidate. The figures I have mentioned are reasonably accurate. I am not including the occasional students, playboys and playgirls, who go along with the party for kicks.

The part of the factory in which I was employed was known as the Hardening Shop. As long as I live, I will never forget it. The furnaces were of the Rotary Hearth type, electrically run with oil and water coolers at the sides. The bearings were hardened and covered with a thin layer of nickel alloy. I became a proficient furnace operator after a few months and was in complete charge of the setting, dismantling, etc. of my own furnace. So did Murphy, Pat

Stack and Grogan. We were all employed now by British Timken.

No Englishman would consider working for long in the Hardening Shop. The heat inside the furnace was never less than 840 degrees and often, for special jobs, as high as 960 degrees. There were five nationalities employed in this part of the factory – Poles, Czechs, Taffies, Jocks and Paddies. There were no Limeys. It's all right to call an Irishman Paddy but it is considered insulting to call an Englishman Limey.

There were three shifts, 6.30 a.m. to 2.30 p.m., 2.30 p.m. to 10 p.m. and 10 p.m. to 6.30 a.m. The money was excellent and if one worked full Saturdays or double shift on Sundays there was an assured minimum wage packet of eighteen pounds a week, often twenty five with double shifts but nobody could stand this for long. Sunday work was difficult but absolutely imperative for married men who would have to send home eight pounds to twelve pounds a week. It meant rising at four a.m., Mass at five a.m., and a three-mile cycle or walk to the factory. A man really enjoyed a few pints when he finished at six o'clock Sunday evening, that is if he didn't have to return to start a night shift at ten o'clock.

There was only one married man in our digs at this time. His wages, with tax deducted, averaged £14 per week. He sent home £8 to a wife and five children. He paid £3 for digs, laundry, repairs etc. Bus fares were £1. This left him £2 for smokes, drinks, clothes and shoe purchases, holiday fund and union fees. He never complained. The important thing was that he could send £8 a week to his wife and children. Most of the married men I knew did not send home this amount and some sent nothing at all after a while. Others took up with new companions and promptly forgot their first marital obligations. Most wives in Ireland are too proud and too fond of their children to do anything about it. Again it is the old, old curse of emigration.

In Ireland there is the same frightening complacency at the same old indignities.

Married men should not be forced to go cringing with their caps in their hands to T.D.'s and County Councillors, looking for jobs. This is all wrong. Applications should be made through the proper channels and a man should be permitted to retain his self-respect and dignity. It is not just, and too often the wrong men get the jobs. Factories and schemes are going ahead with a rare zest in Ireland but again it is the local politician who has the biggest say in the giving of a job. If he has a shop, he'll favour his own customers. If he hasn't he'll favour his own party. Merit is ignored and the claims of good men are laughed off. I could go on for ever!

Around this time in Northampton, encouraged by my fellow-boarders, I wrote another novel. They brought me in pints at night when I refused to leave my writing. It was rejected by several publishers. Poems, stories and essays were being returned by the dozen, as fast as they were written.

I decided to abandon writing and concentrate on my job.

Summer time came and conditions in the factory were bad.

The heat was almost unbearable and I thought longingly of the fresh taunting breezes which laughed around the cliffs and headlands of Ballybunion. At times the fumes from the oil coolers were stifling. This was no way for a man to be wasting his life, I thought, but then, beggars can't be choosers.

A man wore his oily overalls and oily clogs – nothing else. I worked in oily football togs and what a strange sight I must have presented. I weighed about ten stone at the time. I often caught the English foreman looking at me curiously. He had strong doubts about my physical condition, I'm sure. What he didn't know was that I could eat twice as much as he could. It was my length and thinness that confused him.

Beryl Atkinson was good to us in those days. The food was appropriate and our shirts, socks and vests were always immaculately clean. It was a long hot summer and the pace was just about as much as we could manage.

I remember one particularly depressing evening in late May. We arrived home from work exhausted. Luton town were playing the Northampton Cobblers in the park, but none of us had money and we had a tacit agreement about subbing Beryl and 'Enery.

Beryl wore a smug smile when I came in. Then she produced a slim envelope from a pocket of her apron and handed it to me. It was from a woman's magazine and – Holy God! – it contained a cheque for fifteen pounds.

Oh, the joy that was mine at that moment. Murphy hurried upstairs to hide his feelings. Beryl was so overcome that she had to sit down. 'Enery made mysterious noises in the background and my hand was being shaken with great force by my workmates.

That night we dressed up and celebrated the occasion in true style and there was enough left over to purchase eight respectable seats at the Royal for a one-night visit of the Folies Bergère on the following Saturday night.

'Enery and Beryl dressed for the occasion. I have seen musty dress suits in my time but 'Enery's took the biscuit. It was truly the stuff with the green tinge. It was frayed at the sleeves, the pockets and the trousers-ends. It was far too small but he persisted in dressing. His last visit to a theatre was seventeen years before.

Beryl wore a clinging black frock with a flimsy red handkerchief attached.

The show started at eight, but we had no idea as the curtain went up what was in store for us. After a few preliminary cracks by the M.C. the chorus emerged, bare from the waist up. They cavorted about the stage in this condition to the utter astonishment of 'Enery and Beryl. A few more items of the smutty variety and then came the *piece de resistance* of the evening – two female contortionists who, if one were to believe the bills, had shocked London and Paris.

It was while these girls were performing that the unexpected happened. One of the chorus appeared on the stage in her birthday suit. There were loud hysterical screams from backstage. In the front of the house an indignant few stood up and protested. Others hooted and jeered while the majority applauded. The girl was obviously quite drunk and it was certainly not part of the show. She was seized by the contortionists and dragged off the stage. Beryl had a handkerchief over her face. There was a good deal of disorder since the crowd could not be kept under control. There were, however, a few worthwhile scraps at the end of the hall. From the safety of our seven-and-sixpenny seats we urged the opponents to greater efforts. All in all it was a joyful occasion, an unexpectedly hilarious night. After a while the show resumed its mediocre course and closed at the final curtain to a well-pleased house.

That summer of 1952 was an eventful one, apart from the fact that it was the first time I got paid for a piece of writing. It marked the accession of Elizabeth II after the death of George VI. Japan again became a sovereign state. King Farouk abdicated and a state of emergency was proclaimed in Kenya owing to Mau Mau terrorism. Eisenhower was elected to the Presidency of the U.S.A. and Chaim Weisman, the first President of Israel, passed away.

The furnaces of British Timken were never busier than at this time. Murphy got a rupture from lifting crates of steel cones. Pat Stack developed pleurisy and was nursed back to health free of charge by Beryl Atkinson. I had five teeth pulled by a National Health dentist who berated me for spitting blood into a wash-basin specially designed for such post-molar practices. He told me that I should go to bed. I went to bed and, but for the timely arrival of Murphy, the ensuing haemorrhage would have precluded any possibility whatsoever of this biography.

I don't recall which hurling team and football team won the All-Ireland Finals of 1952. We listened to all the provincial finals, semi-finals and All-Irelands over the radio. There were no reports in the English papers of these matches.

We journeyed to London to see a great Irish Rugby fifteen beaten by a flukey try in the snow earlier that year.

G.A.A. fans may wonder why Irishmen like ourselves

58

made this journey. The answer is that Ireland were playing. It was worth it to see green jerseys on the field and worth the whole world to hear other enthusiastic voices like ours raised in a great cry for the sake of sport of all kind and for the strange singular love of our own peculiar country.

Our social life, apart from the week-end visit to the pub, was practically non-existent. We made a few visits to the local Irish club and after a typical Irish row there I was lucky to be alive.

It happened on a Sunday night.

The Irish Club stands next to the Cathedral, a long mournful one-storied hall, used mostly for dancing.

On this night Frank McBride and I, because we had no resources and because we had nothing better to do, decided to while away a few hours there.

We walked from Abingdon Avenue across the park, past the drill-hall, to the respectable residential area where the club stood. There was a dance in full swing when we entered and an Irish girl with an English accent was singing 'The Green Glens of Antrim'. We went straight to the tea-bar. There was no other and if there was we couldn't have mustered the price of a drink between us. Tea was threepence a cup and we ordered two. Just then the bar closed down for the night, possibly because the girl who served wanted to join in the dancing. But at that moment a burly copper-faced youth with a shock of red hair falling down over his eyes called for a cup of tea. The girl explained that the bar was closed. He told her what he thought of her, seized my cup of tea and flung it with shattering force against the back wall just above the girl's head.

Frank McBride promptly intervened, but the youth, who was much stronger and twenty years younger, pushed him so hard that he knocked Frank on the flat of his back. I hauled off and hit the cup-smasher with a straight left on that most sensitive of organs, the nose. He recovered and I nailed him on the same spot again.

Now, there is an old axiom about straight lefts which I have always credited. When on the defensive through no fault of one's own, the sensible tactic is to lead with a good straight left. This should be followed immediately by two more straight lefts. If, however, after the third straight left the recipient comes in for more, the procedure should be to put the straight left into one's pocket and depart the scene as quickly as possible.

In my case, unfortunately, there was no departing the scene. We were surrounded almost immediately by several of my opponent's hunting pack. The battle ranged from one end of the hall to the other. This was by design rather than accident, since McBride and I agreed by the survival instinct to fight an evasive action towards the nearest exit.

Fortunately for McBride he was shielded by a cluster of Northern Ireland women who dragged him into the cloakroom. I deduced that if I got out on the street I could make for the open spaces of Abingdon Park and since I was a better runner than fighter my chances of escape were reasonable.

> *'The best laid schemes of mice and men*
> *Gang aft agley;*
> *And leave us nought but grief and pain*
>   *For promised play...'*

Burns certainly knew his business when he penned those lines.

Outside the door they were waiting for me. A voice somewhere shouted: Fair play!' and another said: Make a ring!' I was dizzy by this time from the showers of glancing blows received during the retreat from the tea-bar. I distinctly remember that there was a momentary silence in the street after the call for 'make a ring.' Some of the crowd drew back and I could see a blonde-haired well-built man in the centre of the roadway with his coat off and his sleeves rolled up. He offered out any man in the crowd. Since I was the only member of the crowd in question this should have struck me as amusing – but it didn't.

I never got as far as my challenger. Blows and kicks came from all sides and the next thing I remembered was waking up two and a half hours later in hospital.

After a week I recovered enough to return to the Atkinsons, who had, together with my fellow-boarders, visited me every day while I was laid up. I spent another week in semi-convalescence before returning to work. During that time I paid a visit to our local National Health doctor. I was a sorry sight.

'How is it,' he said, 'that you Paddies are always knocking each other about?'

'How do you mean?' I asked.

'Why you Irish are always fighting?' he said.

'Fist-fights only!' I said indignantly.

'It's disgraceful!' he said.

'It isn't half as disgraceful as the way you English behave,' I told him.

'Don't be silly,' he said indignantly; 'the English don't behave like that.'

'Ah, come off it,' I said. 'Didn't ye fight with everyone – The Americans, the French, the Spanish, the blacks, the Boers, the Germans, the Dutch, the Irish... I could go on all day.'

He showed me out of his office somewhat coolly.

After Mass the following Sunday I discovered why I wasn't booted to Kingdom Come the night of the fight. After I had been knocked unconscious on the street outside the club a girl from Monaghan threw herself across my head and shoulders when the kicking started. She clung on despite threats and blows, and if she should happen to read this I ask her to get in touch with me without fail.

I don't know a great deal about her. At the time she was a clippie (or bus-conductress). I knew her vaguely by sight. I think her christian name was Chrissie and I know that she hailed from Monaghan. I'm pretty sure that I wouldn't be writing this to-day but for her great Christian impulse. When I called to where she stayed in Northampton her landlady told me that she had gone back to Ireland.

There was also a small man called O'Connor who came from somewhere in the Dingle peninsula. I was told that he leaped into the fray in the latter stages but was beaten down by force of numbers.

To him and to Chrissie, wherever they are, I extend my deepest gratitude and can only pray that they will both get in touch with me.

CHAPTER

V

We steered clear of the Irish Club after that.

We could have retaliated but what would it achieve unless to endorse my medical friend's contention that the Irish were, indeed, always fighting.

Back to the writing again: I couldn't keep away from it. I wrote a short radio play for the B.B.C. which was returned. I wrote a few short stories for Radio Eireann which were also returned. I submitted articles, stories and poems to Irish, American and English periodicals, newspapers and journals – all without success.

Some of the replies were favourable, particularly one from Malcolm Muggeridge, who told me to keep on writing. Another letter from the late Joseph O'Connor, author of 'The Norwayman' and 'Hostage to Fortune' praised a poem of mine which he had read in a newspaper. He too told me to keep on writing no matter what. These letters helped. Everybody – especially an aspirant to the writing trade – likes a pat on the back now and again.

Then one day in the Hardening Shop a man I knew well – we'll call him Marius the Pole for short – dropped dead in front of the furnace where he worked. He was a young man, handsome and unmarried. He was a country boy like myself. He came from near the town of Otwock on the Vistula, about thirty miles from Warsaw. He died a long way from home in a strange land, unloved and unwanted.

Shortly after that – and because of that – I left Northampton on my own and worked for a while as a barman in Leicester and later in London. I saw some good fights between the Teds and the Irish from the not too safe vantage point of behind the counter.

I met and made friends with some wonderful Irishmen during this time. These were a proud resilient kind of men who had taken the knocks of the world in their stride and came up, smiling, for more. They had worked the country from Tynecastle to Southampton. Wherever construction was in progress they were in demand. One look at this type of man and no honest foreman could refuse him work.

They liked to work. They couldn't do without it and they boasted about great feats of tunnel-digging, block-laying and masonry. They were clean men with sunburned faces and mighty brown hands. They were rarely married and they had not seen Ireland for years. Many of them could hardly read but they were knowledgeable men and fit for any company. They used to be known as 'Long-Distance Men' and 'Buck Navvies.' They were a breed apart. They were respected, and even loved, by the English people who knew them. They had hearts of gold and they make a strange contrast to the narrow-trousered perfumed delinquents of to-day. They had their own poets and their own rules about behaviour. Their songs were strong but funny:

> "Twas in the kip at Scunthorpe
> We put down the skillet pot
> And 'ere the stew was halfway through
> We ate the shaggin' lot!"

They have almost disappeared from the scene now and it's a pity because they knew how to work and they gave labour a status which made a profession look like a pastime.

As a barman I found little time for writing. There was always time for drinking and reminiscing but this period was the most important in my development as a writer. I lost objectivity and became involved personally with human beings. To involve oneself is a dangerous game but I was lucky and emerged without loss of inner face or sense of obligation. I was growing wiser too – if any man of twenty three is wise. I took long week-ends off to see the country. Coach tours were the most comfortable and the most informative. The rolling English countryside is easily absorbed but it cannot compete with the savage grandeur of Irish scenery – or so my prejudice says. After several weeks as a barman and two spent harvesting with farmers, I returned again to Northampton.

The heat of the heavy summer had passed and I returned to the furnaces. Pat Stack had left England and gone to Dublin in search of a job. When we heard from him again he was in Canada in the Arctic circle, driving a bulldozer. An article of his appeared in the 'Canadian Digest' about two years ago. Maybe it was my influence! The last I heard from him, he had just returned from an expedition to Devon Island which is about seventy eight degrees north on the end of the North West Territory. It was organised by the Arctic Institute of North America and financed by the National Geographic Society for the purpose of studying Oceanography, Glaceology, and Meteorology. He was the only Irishman on the twelve-man team. Another distinguished member of the expedition, who is at present studying at Oxford, was Charles Shackleton, grandson of the great Antarctic explorer. Temperatures were forty and fifty degrees below freezing point in winter. A far cry from the furnaces of British Timken but then I remember Pat Stack telling me once: 'If I ever get out of this hell hole I won't be seen within a thousand miles of heat again!'.

Pat had a wonderful sense of humour. It was he who convinced Beryl Atkinson that leprechauns really existed back in Ireland. 'I often saw leprechaun's droppings,' he told her, 'when I was out pickin' mushrooms in the morning'.

Towards the end of Autumn I got an irrepressible longing for home. I was corresponding regularly with Mary and we both agreed that I should come back. We could consider emigrating to America if all fruit failed in my native land. I had a little money, not a great deal – a few hundred pounds hard earned – but I was in love and I was learning how to write.

I made up my mind to get back to Ireland by hook or by crook.

When you're a buck-navvy in Britain, it's next to impossible to get a job in Ireland.

My pharmaceutical background was of considerable help to me and one morning I saw what I wanted in an Irish paper. It was one of the usual advertisements one sees on the back pages, a vacancy for a travelling salesman. No previous experience was required. Intending applicants should possess the leaving certificate and have at least one year's experience of selling in a retail pharmacy. The age bracket was twenty-one to twenty-five.

I took some time off from work and journeyed to Dublin for the interview. Mary came up from Kerry to meet me and we spent a few enjoyable days in the metropolis.

But about the vacant position. A letter from the company dictated that I present myself at a certain hotel where I was to produce references and render an account of myself. I rose early on the appointed morning, shaved carefully, donned my best shirt and tie and my best suit. The other one was unfit for social occasions. Mary and I went to Mass and breakfasted, after which I set out for the hotel and for whatever fate awaited me.

I was uncertain and nervous. I popped into a pub en route and swallowed a large whiskey which steadied me considerably. I also had the foresight to purchase a tuppeny packet of mints. At the hotel I was shown into a small ante-room and told to wait. After several minutes a young man emerged from the interrogating chamber. He was about the same age as myself. He wore a puzzled look on his face. When he saw me he stopped.

'What games do you play?' he asked.

'What do you want to know for?' I said.

'Look!' he said, 'your man in there asked me the same question and I told him I played football and snooker. He didn't seem to approve. My advice to you is cricket at least.'

I thanked him and he exited with a magnanimous wave of the hand.

After a few moments an immaculately-dressed man of forty beckoned to me and I followed him into a staid room which contained a table and two chairs. He took up his position behind the table. coughed and thumbed through several typewritten pages. Attached to one sheet were my references. He motioned me into the other chair and quizzed me briefly about certain aspects of the pharmaceutical trade. I answered the questions easily enough. I felt somehow that I was not making the necessary impact. I discovered later that the job had been given away beforehand. He asked me what schools I had attended. I told him and whilst he did not register any noticeable change I could sense that he was not impressed. I saw my chances of the job flying out the window.

'Why did you ask that question?' I asked politely.

'What question?'

'Where I went to school?'

'We ask everybody,' he said evenly.

'Does it make any difference?' I asked.

He did not see fit to answer that one. Instead he asked me what games I played.

'Russian roulette and pickie,' I said, with what I hoped was contempt.

He did not smile. He terminated the interview by telling me that I would hear from him. I never did.

It was terribly disappointing and so once more I returned to England and Mary returned to Kerry. What a pity the fraud who interviewed me could not be forced to spend a few weeks in the hardening shop of British Timken!

Back in Northampton I bought the Irish papers every day and studied the 'Positions Vacant' columns assiduously. Most of the jobs had gone by the time my letters reached their Irish destinations. Then, one day, in the 'Irish Independent' I saw an advertisement announcing a vacancy for a chemist's assistant in the village of Doneraile in County Cork. I applied and, to my astonishment, was accepted by return of post. I was to report for work in two weeks. The wages were £ 2.10.0 per week indoor. There weren't many applicants for that kind of money. In fact there wasn't any other. Anyway I was thankful for the chance to return and it was at least a beginning. I gave notice to my employers and informed 'Enery and Beryl of my plans. There was a farewell party at 'The Black Boy', some weeping and much drinking.

So, after a two-years sojourn as a buck-navvy I found myself back in Ireland again, one of the lucky ones. Neither Camden Town nor Cricklewood stole my youth away even if they did steal other things.

On my way home I saw the young red-faced Paddies and the glowing childish Biddies, with their cheap brown suitcases boarding the train at Limerick, bound for Dun Laoghaire. 'May God keep you,' I said to myself, 'you luckless wretches. What an awful inheritance is yours?'

'Oh, Camden Town, Oh Camden Town, you stole my youth away;
For I was young and innocent and you were old and grey!'

In Doneraile, of course, I wrote another novel. It went its merry rounds and came back to me again, rejected. The old man for whom I worked in Doneraile is now dead. He was ninety-three then and as hardy as a leveret. He was a freemason and one of the world's leading authorities on antique silver. When he died he left a quarter of a million pounds behind him. The housekeeper was seventy-five and I was twenty-four. The shop was situated on the main street and part of my job was to attend antique petrol pumps which stood outside the door. This I did not mind so much, but there was something else which annoyed me no end. Doneraile was, and still is, one of the last bastions of the ascendancy class. Lying in the heart of the Duhallow country it is surrounded by fertile fields as far as the eye can see. No question about it, but the English certainly picked the best of it for themselves and left us the bogs and the hills. Most of the local gentry were retired brigadiers, majors, captains, lords, knights and what-have you. They did not mix with the locals. When they came to shop in jeeps and cars, they pulled up outside the shop and hooted. Immediately the shopkeeper rushed out to see what they wanted. I had thought that all that sort of thing had disappeared with the civil war, but I was wrong. Respect and courtesy are prizeworthy traits but servility is a horse of a different colour. To their credit, many of the shopkeepers stayed behind their counters and waited for the so-called gentry to come in. The lesser of the class, such as the mere honourables were just as bad. The honourable so-and-so by name maybe but just the same as the rest of us by nature. Their accents were the last word in affectation. I always thought a 'caw' was something a crow said, but there are also such things as motor-caws. The townspeople themselves were friendly and generous and, above all, good-humoured.

The house where I resided was like a museum. The contents realised a fabulous sum when the old man died.

One room was crammed from floor to ceiling with silver plate, cups, statuettes and any other ornament you care to imagine; there was even a silver chamber-pot. Another room was packed with valuable books and another with paintings.

Another house in the town, owned by the old man, was filled with antique furniture. He never missed an auction whether it was in Ballinasloe or Dunmore East.

My duties in the shop were few. There was a pile ointment which had to be made up regularly for the late Lord Doneraile, and the packaging of a scour powder which the old man had himself invented.

This was internationally famous and to the public known as 'Jones' Scour Specific.' It is not much in demand nowadays but there was a time, before the advent of more modern drugs, when he disposed of tens of thousands of packages every year. He made up the powder himself, in a cement-mixer and nobody was acquainted with the ingredients. It was easy to guess the identities of the powders which made up the mixture, but local belief held that there was a tiny package of some mysterious white powder procured from secret Duhallow herbs which was added to every thousand pounds of the powder. Orders used to come from places as far away as Venezuela, South Africa and New Zealand and there was no question but that it was a relatively effective treatment for white scour in calves.

Here again the food left a lot to be desired but occasionally there was a rare treat for tea – a slice or two of brawn or German sausage – but no machine that I know of could cut such paper-thin slices. A pound of brawn went a long way and an assistant, who went before me, was known to say that he could have papered his bedroom with a pound of it. But for the kindness of neighbours, who supplied me with late-night mugs of excellent soup and frequent repasts of cold pig's head, this starvation diet would have been intolerable.

In Doneraile I met the man who was to be one of my closest friends. He was a State forester. He still is. His name is Batt Crowley and he is from the stony County of Clare. I named my most recent play after him – 'The Man from Clare.' Till the day I die I will never forget one particular feed of roast goose which I ate in his house. He was unlucky enough to be state forester in Doneraile during the notorious Streamhill forest fire, one of the biggest this country has ever known. Five hundred troops and hundreds of local volunteers were called upon to quell the spread and I myself was a volunteer firefighter for a night and a day. I was afterwards fully compensated by the Department for my time and labour. So was everybody else who took part. There was even porter available for those who felt in need of it.

Batt Crowley showed a keen interest in my writing when nobody else did. He made me write another novel, and he was responsible for making me write my first play – a one-act whose title I have forgotten. Repeatedly he told me that my strength lay in development of characters, but around this time the Kelliher Shield and the Cork County Football Championship were in full swing so Crowley came out of retirement and we both played with Fermoy.

It was an enjoyable season and we beat the Civic Guards

in the second round of the championship – at football, of course. That was as far as we got. There followed an uneventful summer in that drowsiest of peaceful villages, a summer of long walks and longer conversations and making friends with country people. There was little drinking except on Sunday nights, but the problem here was the Civic Guards who would walk up and down the main street when the crowds gathered. They often turned a blind eye and the patrons entered the licensed premises, but sometimes there were raids although I was never caught in one of these. Some narrow escapes, yes, but a natural agility is a blessing in public-house escapades, and a glib tongue with a soft-hearted sergeant is of inestimable value when a man is caught climbing out of a back window with a pint in his hand.

After the better part of a year in Doneraile, I grew restive again and began to make plans for America. There was no future in £2.10.0 a week indoor. I contacted an Aunt of mine in America and arranged to have her claim me. Mary would follow, or if possible we would leave together.

Towards the end of the year, however, my first boss in Listowel wrote offering me a decent job which I gladly accepted. I had a final disagreement with my Doneraile governor concerning holiday pay – a commodity he had never heard of, or so at least he told me. He considered it a downright impertinence and told me, that he, himself, never took a holiday in his life. I never doubted it. His quarter-million pound fortune was all the proof I needed. He refused to pay me. The amount was only a few pounds, but he could be just as adamant over a few pence. In the

73

end, after various veiled threats about litigation, he compromised and paid me half of the amount involved, or to be exact £ 2.5.0.

Back to Listowel again and now on the lookout for a house where I could set up some sort of business. It was my intention to start a small bookshop and keep my job as well but, as it turned out, things did not work out that way and eventually we bought a public-house. We borrowed most of the money from an obliging bank-manager and hoped for the best.

On January 5th of 1955, Mary and I were married in Knocknagoshel Church. The roads were covered with snow that morning and traffic was at a standstill almost everywhere but we were married on time.

CHAPTER

VI

I was the first of my family to marry, but naturally not the last.

It was an enjoyable wedding, as weddings go. The honeymoon didn't last as long as we would like but it lasted long enough. In our grandparents' time there was no such thing as a honeymoon. They got married, had the reception at the bride's home, popped into bed in their own home, and that was that. I heard of one couple who didn't go to bed at all but waited up most of the night eating blackcurrant jam left over from the day's feasting. Anyhow, if it's any consolation to those who have had no honeymoons, statistics show that only 20% of the world's population goes honeymooning at this present time and of that 20% only 2% can afford it. In fact only about 5% of people can afford to marry at all which is as good a reason as any for marrying.

In the pub we had to work hard to pay back the money we had borrowed. We would open at nine o'clock in the morning and close around twelve o'clock at night. Sunday nights were the best for business. At that time Sunday opening was not permitted and if a licencee was foolish enough to be caught, he was generally fined and upbraided by the justice. He always pleaded guilty. A not-guilty plea was unheard of and would have upset the whole judiciary system in respect of the licensing laws.

Publicans, though no fault of their own, had no respect whatsoever for the licensing laws. Most of the drinking was done by night and particularly on Sunday nights when the country people came into town for a few pints. Certain pubs stayed open till all hours of the morning because there was no business by day. There is a famous story told about a temperate tourist who was walking up the Main street in Ballybunion some years ago. He was appalled to see men leaving licensed premises when the law prescribed otherwise. He approached a Civic Guard who stood nonchalantly at a nearly corner.

'Could you tell me,' he asked, 'what time the pubs close here?'

The Guard scratched his head for a moment in deliberation:

'Shortly after the Listowel Races, sir,' he said, 'out in the middle of October.'

The old licensing laws were unbelievably stupid and obsolete and if it is any information to those who object to Sunday drinking, there was twice the amount of liquor consumed when it was illegal to do so.

In Listowel at that time most pubs which did a brisk Sunday night business employed a lookout man. Entry to the pub was usually through the back door, since the Civic Guards paraded the streets regularly. A good lookout man was worth his weight in gold and I was lucky to find a really brilliant exponent of this little-known art. His name was Jimmy Joy – the Lord have mercy on him. He could literally smell Guards but I have a sneaking suspicion that they gave him a good deel of leeway as long as he didn't overdo it. Most sensible Superintendents and Sergeants realised that the Sunday night business was the bread and butter of the small pubs and they raided only when it was absolutely necessary.

On Sunday nights admission to our pub was by the back gate which opened on to a backway affording two means of escape. Whenever there was a knock at the timber door – one rap, a pause and two more raps – Jimmy would kneel down and peep under the door. If the knocker wore brown shoes he was admitted immediately. No Guard wears brown shoes when on duty. If the knocker wore black shoes further investigation was necessary. If the knocker had folds on his trousers all was well. The pants of a Guard's uniform are without folds.

When the Guards raided, Jimmy usually spoke like an old woman. To the first official knock he would ask in a high-pitched tremulous tone: 'Who's that?'

'Guards on publichouse duty!' would come the answer.

'There's no one here, sir!' Jimmy would reply in his old woman's voice.

'Open up, please!' the Guard would insist.

'I can't, sir. I'm in my shift!' Jimmy would cry.

This worked a few times, but sometimes the Guards meant business. If the raid was a token raid only one Guard was on duty. He would knock at the back door announcing that he was a Guard on publichouse duty. He was stalled until such time as all the customers got out the front door. If he knocked at the front door everybody got away through the back door.

When two Guards were on duty, one at the front door and one at the back, the jig was up. The customers were hurried upstairs to the bathroom, bedroom, sitting room –

any place where they could hide until the raid was over. The toilet was the best place to hide during a raid! All men have respect for the privacy of their fellows.

When the Guards were admitted, the Sergeant might say offhand: 'Nice bit of an evening, John, thank God!' The bar would generally be reeking with tobacco smoke and fumes of porter. If there wasn't time to go ret rid of them there might be a few half-filled pints on the counter.

'Anybody on the premises?'

'Devil a one, Sergeant!'

Sometimes the raid would end here, but there were some times when the Guards went further. Justifiable letters from angry wives about husbands who were spending their wages or letters from jealous girlfriends left the Sergant or the Guards no option.

'Is there anyone upstairs?'

'There's two or three, Sergeant!' There might be anything from forty to a hundred up there.

'I'll go up,' the Sergeant would say.

'Yerra, don't bother, Sergeant. I'll go up and bring them down for you!'

Upstairs, some of the boys were in bed with their clothes on. Others hid in wardrobes, or under beds. The toilet was crammed to capacity and the door was locked from within.

'There's a raid on, lads,' I called. 'How about a few volunteers?'

A moment's pause and three men came forward from their respective hiding-places. I can't remember now who the first two were, but the third was Dickeen Roche. He could move about freely at that time, with the aid of a stick.

He's confined to a wheelchair now and totally crippled with arthritis. Downstairs – to face the sergeant.

'Is that the lot?' from the sergeant.

'This is the lot, sergeant!'

The sergeant looked them over.

'A likely-looking bunch,' he says. 'Alright, how can you account for your presence on these premises?'

'I was dry, sir,' from the first.

'All I was drinkin' was minerals,' from the second.

'Guilty, but insane, sergeant,' says Dickeen Roche.

The sergeant proceeds to take their names and tells them that they should be ashamed of themselves.

They were not all like the sergeant – although the majority were. I remember one night we were raided by two new arrivals. They captured the entire company with one exception. On their way out they nabbed a man called Dinny Connor at the back gate. It was very dark and I wasn't in the house at the time.

'How can *you* account for being on the premises?'

'I'm John B.,' says Dinny, shaking both their hands and welcoming them to Listowel.

As I've said, it wasn't all apple-pie. I remember another occasion when Mary was in the nursing home after our second boy was born. It was two-thirty in the morning and I was writing. Loud knocking at the door. I ignored it at first, thinking it might be some thirsty soul who had seen my light. The knocking persisted and I went to see who it was. Two young guards.

'What's up?' I asked.

'Guards on duty,' one of them said matter of factly.

'There's nobody here,' I said, 'and I'm in the middle of a piece of writing.'

They insisted upon entering. I turned on the light in the shop, but that wasn't enough. They demanded that I allow them upstairs.

'It's going on for three o'clock,' I explained. 'There's nobody there but a younger brother of mine, Denis; the girl who works in the house, and the baby.'

They had their way and up they went.

'Who's in there?' one of them asked.

'Brother,' I told him.

They entered without knocking and shone the light on his face. He woke up, pulled on his pants and got up. They demanded his name and he told them. On to the toilet. Nobody there. The upstairs kitchen. Nobody there. The sitting room. Nobody there.

'What's in here?' they asked when they came to the room where the girl and the baby slept. I told them. Again one of them entered without knocking, and shone the light on the girl's face. She stirred in her sleep and woke up, rubbing her eyes, very frightened. He then shone the light into the baby's cot but the child didn't wake up. We then asked them to leave the premises, which they did with rather bad grace and deliberate slowness. On the way out I said to the man with the torch: 'You're a lucky man that child didn't wake up.'

In the street, they stood outside the door for over an hour. The girl got up and made some tea. I could never discover the motive for this raid. Perhaps it was a diversion to while away a few of the night's lonely hours. These contemptible curs were a disgrace to a decent body of men with an honourable reputation. Naturally enough there is still a good deal of resentment among small-town publicans because of the Guards' behaviour. Some overdid their duties and exhibited a shocking lack of taste and courtesy. The vast majority were a credit to their communities, but there were too many instances like mine. In justice to the Guards, however, it must be said that the archaic licensing laws were the root cause of resentment. The government availed of the illicit taxes collected after hours. The government was fully aware that after-hours drinking was going on and many of its members were themselves publicans. Many more were expert at whiskey and brandy slugging and one could wish for no better customers after hours.

The new licencing laws are good but it is hard on small family pubs which are run by one man and his wife. They work for a bare livelihood from 10.30 a.m. till 11.40 p.m. six days of the week and on the seventh, the holy Sabbath, they work from 12 noon till 2 p.m. and again from 4 p.m. till ten past ten at night. There is no state pension for the publican when he gets old, despite his being the country's greatest tax-gatherer, despite his having no half-day, no Sunday off, no holiday of any kind with the isolated exceptions of Christmas Day and Good Friday and even on these days the small rural publican, who is really dependent upon the pub for his living, is not free. His regular customers will ask him to let them in for a few hours and this is a terrible quandary. If he tells them he can't because it's Christmas and he wants the day for himself and his family, there is always the danger that they will go elsewhere and, once gone, they might stay away for good.

It happens all the time and if there is a more precarious living I would like to hear of it. Then there are the other dangers, the danger from assault by drunks who have a grudge against the world. We read about it in the papers every day. A publican has the power to refuse any man for a drink if he doesn't like his face, manner or general attitude. People don't realise this and when they are refused a drink their ire is aroused and there is a tendency to beat up the publican, particularly if he is an oldish or weak man who cannot defend himself.

It happened to myself one night after a football match. I was leaving out five men one night when one of them suddenly remembered that he owed me a hiding because of some remark I once passed to him after a football game. I had completely forgotten about it. There was nobody else in the house at the time. Mary was in bed, and they gathered around me in the backyard.

The same group had rows in every pub they ever entered.

They made a rather serious mistake this time. An old friend of mine was passing down the back-lane on his way for a pint and he heard the commotion. I got the back gate opened for him and he stormed in. He is a farmer's son, weighs about fifteen stone and stands about six feet two inches in his socks. It reminded me of Cuchullain breaking his bonds.

We got them out, and it was a pleasure to stand him a pint. I was very lucky that he happened along when he did. He was on his way home when the thought struck him: 'I'll call to John B's for a pint.' If he hadn't come along and if those cowardly whelps had got me down, God only knows what would have happened. But such are the fortunes of war or rather the fortunes of publichouse keeping. Most of the publicans I know have been beaten up at one time or another, for no reason whatsoever. It is an occupational hazard. Yet when missionaries come to town during retreats and missions they unfailingly attack publicans. They forget that God created publicans, too, and that publicans have the same rights as other citizens. They are as honest and as good morally as any other citizen. Not all publicans are perfect. Not all men are perfect. No man is perfect.

I would not advise anybody to become a publican, and I mean this from my heart. My own wife was advised, as a schoolgirl, by her nuns: 'Never marry a publican.' The nuns knew what they were talking about, because a pub is not a home. It is a public house where any kind of scoundrel can enter and spend his time. A man can bore you to death if he wants to and you have to hear his confession too if he feels like telling it. You have to listen to best friends cutting each other to pieces when one or the other is absent. You have to listen to foul gossip of every description or go out of business. You have to listen to every dirty story that goes the rounds. This is not so bad since most of us enjoy a spicy story but it is the re-telling tens of times that irritates you and you have to laugh as much as you did when you heard it the first time or you'll find yourself losing customers.

After two years in the pub I started to write again. I would begin at twelve o'clock at night when all the customers had departed. I'd fill a pint and draw the table near to the fire. I started with short stories and poems and I would write till three or four o'clock in the morning, writing a thousand words an hour and drinking a pint every hour, maybe boiling three or four hardboiled eggs if the hunger was prodding me. Sometimes the Guards would raid when they saw the light but they were civil and kind and they never knocked when they found out what I was trying to do. I used up a lot of sixpenny notebooks. I'm a poor typist but in the next street is a professional who does all my typing for me.

All the poems came back, and all the stories. I had stacks of rejection slips. In the first year I must have sent away fifty poems and a hundred stories. 'The Evening Press' did purchase one about an Inspector Blunt who could tell by picking a hair from the ground that its owner was possessed of buck teeth and disliked garlic. They asked me for more along the same lines, but these must have been too nonsensical because they returned them.

One night, around the fire in the back kitchen, a friend suggested that I write to a Correspondence School where they teach people how to produce marketable writing. I almost did, but I discussed it with Dickeen Roche and the boys and we reached certain conclusions. Dickeen was in his wheelchair at this time and a pillar of wisdom though buttressed by enormous slabs of humour. Jack Duggan sat in the corner, smoking his pipe and holding forth from the experience of his seventy-five years. Rumour has it that he drank 1,500 half-tierces of porter in his lifetime yet he was never seen drunk, his family were a credit to him and he never missed a day's work.

Why did these people not write stories themselves if there was all the money they promised to be made from it?

'It's the same as the Crosswords,' Dickeen Roche said. 'They'll sell you books telling you how to win, but have they won themselves?'

Jack Duggan finished his pint and stroked his moustache. 'Or tips for horses,' he said. 'I paid a shilling for three tips at Listowel Races and the three of them were down the field.'

'That is correct!' Roger True Blue said, shifting his weight on the chair and winking at Dickeen Roche.

'Stick to your guns,' Dickeen said, 'and don't be putting in any big words.'

Everybody agreed that big words were a waste.

'Spell 'tapioca'?' said Roger out of the blue to Jack Duggan.

'I wouldn't eat it if I was paid!' Jack replies.

'Is tapioca good for a fella?' Dickeen asks of Sonny Canavan.

'Anything is good in moderation,' Sonny Canavan replies and calls for four more pints of porter and a half whiskey for Dickeen Roche.

'That we might never lose the tooth for it,' Roger True Blue says.

Roger fooled us all recently by going off it. He hasn't tasted a drink nor smoked a cigarette in the last ten months but he still comes in for a chat or to enquire about Dickeen's garden.

Then one night, after a particularly enjoyable sing-song, when my contribution was a mime of a youngster arriving in London for the first time and returning home a fully-qualified Teddy-boy three months later, Dickeen Roche made the following prophetic announcement:

'Johneen,' he said, you should write a play. You're a shaggin' pantomime!'

CHAPTER

VII

I wrote a three-act play in a few months and I called it 'Barbara Shearing'.

I submitted it to Radio Eireann and it was accepted, subject to a certain amount of re-writing. It was then adapted for radio and it proved a highly successful diversion but it was only a diversion and it lacked depth.

Before it was heard over the Radio, however, I went one night with Mary to see the Listowel Drama Group in 'All Souls' Night' by Joseph Tomelty. I was impressed and, as far as I can remember, it was the first full-length play of consequence I had seen up till then. When I came home that night I was impatient and full of ideas. I sent Mary to bed and filled a pint. I sat by the fire for a while and after a quarter of an hour I reached for my copy-book and pencil.

I started to write and six hours later, or precisely at 6.30 a.m., I had written the first scene of 'Sive'.

I didn't think a whole lot of what I had written and I very nearly crumpled the crammed sheets and tossed them into the fire. Lucky for me, I didn't. About a fortnight later I had completed the first draft of 'Sive'. I showed it to a few people I knew and their opinion was the same. It wouldn't work. For one thing, the names of the characters were nothing short of ludicrous, the theme was outworn and the language too flowery.

I went through the play a second time, and submitted it to the Abbey Theatre. About five weeks later it was returned to me without a word of any kind. I left it lying dead for a few weeks and would have forgotten about it but for a conversation I had with Billy Kearney of the Listowel Drama Group. He suggested that I give it to him to read. I did and he liked it.

Listowel Drama Group were interested. They planned two plays for the following season, and mine was to be one. Bill Kearney sent the play to Micheal O h-Aodha of Radio Eireann. He wrote back immediately and stated that he would do it over the radio. He made a few sensible suggestions and wrote that if the Listowel Drama Group produced 'Sive' it would be the greatest thing that ever happened to amateur drama in Ireland. Frankly, I didn't think so. Neither did anybody else, although we had a certain amount of faith in the play.

Brendan Carroll of Listowel was the producer. He certainly worked hard on the production and anybody who has seen the Listowel Drama Group in Brendan Carroll's production will never forget it.

I am deeply indebted to the Listowel players. They were the first English-speaking amateur group to appear on the Abbey stage. They packed the Abbey for a week, during a heat wave. They were a credit to Listowel and to the amateur drama movement. In a sense they made history and they deserve a special place in the history of Irish theatre.

'Sive' goes on in New York soon and I have been invited to help with its production and to make a few television appearances to assist the publicity end. I haven't made up my mind whether I'll go or not. If I want the play to succeed I must go, but I am not keen on an enforced absence from home. My limit is a week-end in Dublin. Even Belfast gives me the willies and anyway, from what I gather, it is extremely difficult to come across a good pint in New York.

'Sive' was produced there, of course, before and highly successfully at that, in the St. Nicholas of Tolentine auditorium. Some of the narrowbacks didn't like it but the reviews were unanimously good. An off-Broadway production of 'Sive' is an entirely different kettle of fish and an author's presence is essential if he doesn't want his work mutilated and misinterpreted.

It is difficult to make a decision. I would be away for ten or twelve weeks. No friend can advise. It is up to myself.

But back to 'Sive' and Listowel. The Listowel Drama Group won the All-Ireland Amateur Drama Final in Athlone and the much-sought Esso trophy for the first time. They also did the play over Radio Eireann and some members of the cast, together with myself and my brother Eamonn, made a long-playing record of it. All good times must come to an end and the inevitable split broke the Listowel Drama Group into two fair halves. The breach has not been healed to date. The new group call themselves The Listowel Players and I am their patron. I never thought I'd see the day I'd be patron of anything. One schoolmaster predicted the gallows.

It is easy to say to whom it is I owe my success as a writer: to my wife for her constant help, but most of all to my father, – God rest him – because it was he who encouraged me from beginning to end, who edited my early work and gave me the freedom of a fine library, who promised me that if I persevered I would emerge one day as a writer.

January of 1960 was outstanding for little except that a second son was born to us, Conor Anthony. He weighed 7 lbs. 6 oz., had black hair and an appalling voice which he still uses to his own advantage at all hours of the morning.

One bleak day at the beginning of the month, Nora Relihan of the Listowel Players came to me and announced that she intended doing a limited tour with 'Sive'. Nothing could be more agreeable, since she knew the play and royalties are always acceptable.

There was only one fly in the ointment. Nobody could be found to play the part of Carthalawn, the singing tinker, and a conspiracy was instituted without my knowledge. The outcome was that I found myself with a tambourine in my hand and a hat on my head!

The tour was to begin in Ballylongford and end in Castleisland. The profits – if any – were to be used for that most commendable of all purposes, distribution among the players themselves, although we gave the proceeds of a few performances to the Foreign Missions.

The opening night in Ballylongford was memorable. One of the cast, who had never appeared on a stage before, sat too heavily on a naggin of whiskey which rested in the back pocket of his trousers. He did not sit down once during the entire performance. This, however, was far from being the highlight of the night, because I myself gave a performance which is still spoken of in Ballylongford.

Shortly before I exited in the second act, having sung my ballad, I felt a sudden loosening around the waist of my trousers. It was a borrowed pants with holes in the knees and without buttons. I knew that if I moved the trousers would come down around my ankles. I stood there for several seconds after my father, Pats Bocock, had departed. An urgent voice from the wings came to me clearly:

'Get off the stage, you eejit!'

Still I did not move. The players whispered at me in desperation to get the hell out of it, but nothing doing! I decided to sing another verse of the ballad. The minute I lifted my hand to strike the bodhran, the trousers came down!

Some of the audience thought it was a part of the show and applauded lustily. A few booed and jeered while the remainder stamped their feet. A quick exit from anywhere is physically impossible when one's trousers is down. I shuffled off the stage in disgrace, as fast as I could. When I reappeared in the last act, I was cheered to an echo.

On the second night in Ballylongford the play got off to a flying start and was going like a bomb up until the time of Nanna Glavin's entrance. There was, unfortunately, no sign whatever of Nanna Glavin! Silence on the stage. Unrest among the members of the audience. We found Nanna, after a five minute search, drinking tea out of a flask outside the back entrance to the hall.

During the tour, Nora Relihan was within three months of her second child but she insisted on playing, nevertheless. She always gave a tremendous performance. Whether at the Abbey, the Olympia, or Knocknagoshel she always managed to reach the same high level but Castleisland went near being her undoing.

We were playing to a packed house when midway

through the second act catastrophe struck. Her right leg and thigh completely disappeared. A loose board was responsible. Before any of us could move she had extricated herself and was on her feet in a second. She replaced the offending board and went on with her performance as if nothing had happened. Three months afterwards she had her baby and nobody can blame her if she didn't call the child 'Sive'.

Touring with a play or a show can be good fun provided the audiences behave themselves. One night a man stood up in the second row and wanted to go on the stage to choke Mena Glavin.

'I'll choke her!' he shouted. 'I'll choke her if I get my hands on her!'

Some others resented 'Sive', said it was blasphemous and ungodly, and noisily gave vent to their opinions while the play was in progress. Some – the more sanctimonious – even waited till the show was over and tackled us as we left the hall. One night we were pelted with clods and small stones and one of the girls got a nasty cut in the neck. One outspoken cleric refused to give permission to lease the hall, and even went so far as to tell his flock to shun us. Our greatest enemies were those who hadn't see the play or read it. If we entered a pub after the show some annoyed party was bound to approach us and accuse us of pornography.

'Have you seen the show?' somebody would ask.

'No, and I don't want to!'

'Have you read the play?'

'No, I couldn't read such a filthy thing!'

'But how do you know it's filthy, if you haven't seen it or read it?'

'I don't have to! 'Tis all about bastards, isn't it?'

We spent a week-end in Dingle and got a reception which was nothing short of fantastic especially since we had been told that no plays were supported in Dingle. All in all, the tour was a financial success. We'll allow the critics to assess the artistic side of it. Whatever chance a writer has of getting a good review in the London 'Times' or 'The Herald Tribune,' he has no chance at all in a provincial paper.

Taking all things into consideration, 'Sive' was a success. It had taken twenty years to discover that I could write something marketable. Maybe twenty more will pass before I can say to myself: 'You can write all right. You're O.K. You're a writer!'

CHAPTER

VIII

People will find it hard to understand the strange ambition of a writer.

Ambition is hardly the right word. Search for fulfilment or expression covers it better. It isn't easy to become a writer, particularly a play writer. Anyhow, there is no such thing as the perfect play, or, for that matter, the perfect anything. Anything that is conceived by a human being is no better, or no worse, than the human being.

Nobody ever accepts a writer. He accepts himself. To be a writer, a recognised writer, you have to dream about it from the age of reason onwards. You have to hold this thing into yourself and you have to listen to taunts and jibes far removed from clinical and detached criticism. You have to be conscious of jealousies and the criticism that arises from them but you have to have the consciousness to realise that you are not without jealousy yourself. It is being eternally conscious of oneself that develops the writer.

You have to suffer punches from behind, in the shape of lies and anonymous letters, all delivered by unknown. assailants for tragic reasons known only to themselves. You have to listen to, and read, things about yourself far removed from the truth and you must say nothing whatsoever about it. You'll be called anything from communist to anticlerical and if you dare to deny it you succeed only in hanging yourself.

You have to perpetually preach the gospel of charity to

yourself and, most important of all, whether they be friends or enemies, you have to feel deeply for the hurt in other people. You never stop making allowances, if that is possible. You hope that some day a budding, blossoming writer will come along and say: 'Friends, listen to this! Listen to what this fellow wrote!' and hope that one out of a throng of people will later acknowledge and receipt the quoted comments by writing something better in the same vein himself.

I have always wanted to be a writer. I have needed to be accepted as a writer at any level. It doesn't matter so much now because I am beginning to accept myself. I have lived with other writers – not with their beings but with their books and with their poems, with their plays, essays and journals. To me writing matters, because I believe that it can be the most ennobling profession of all. It is the last of the free professions and a man doesn't need Leaving Cert. or Matriculation to enter it. All he needs is heart, guts, courage, and never to be ashamed of himself or of his own people.

A writer isn't a freak, a man to be watched or made suspect. He is a human being with one of the finest of God's gifts at his disposal – the power to convey the great joys, the great sorrows, the great madnesses and the great hurts in himself and others.

I am a kind of writer. Nobody knows what kind of writer I am, least of all myself. My ambition is that people will say, some time: 'He was a kind of writer. He said things a different way from others.'

Nowadays, unfortunately, it is not enough to write. You

must be a likeable fellow, too. It is almost necessary to be a hypocrite. What I mean is that people who have met you must leave you, saying: 'My God! isn't he a most unassuming fellow!' or: 'He's just like ourselves!' Well, he's not like yourselves, because no two people are alike.

It isn't enough to be a successful writer, any more. You must be a nice likeable fellow, too. But writers can no more be plausible than anybody else. His head is crammed with the seedlings of ideas. A writer gets an idea every day of his life, and he is subject, too, like other human beings, to the occasional retarding obsession, to the waylaying and seductive external influences.

> *'For we are tired of meanings dimed by placid phrases*
> *Wearied of all thinking and its philosophic mazes*
> *Jargons of the tongues have foiled the great expression*
> *And beauty ever pleasing has but kept us in procession.'*

As Dickeen Roche says: 'The more you think about it, the less you're able to think about it!'

The easiest and the surest way of expressing real values is to hug the rails of truth and to hell with those who prefer the diplomacy of justifiable lying.

But the truth is the hardest thing of all to write. There are too many past liaisons, when I personally face the moment of truth or have to make decisions about truth, too many sins committed, too many past ordeals resulting in the nowaday blush, too many occasions of weakness which could all contrive to hang a man. All these manage to blackmail the mind, to obscure the courageous truth which everyman longs to express but daren't. But, thanks to God! you can't blackmail the heart, no matter how hard one tries, because the heart has great moments of love and honesty and great moments of truth and beauty.

But I'm losing sight of my story and now for a word on anonymous letters and their writers, those who are attracted by exaggerated names and circumstances.

I receive about thirty anonymous letters every year but then, who hasn't received an anonymous letter?

I have often asked myself what prompts people to write anonymous letters: why people should deliberately set out to hurt other people who have done them no harm.

Some months ago, Paddy O'Keeffe, Editor of the Farmer's Journal, received an anonymous letter beseeching him not to publish my story in the Journal. He did exactly what one would expect of him – sent the letter along directly to me. I don't know who wrote it. I suppose I could find out easily enough if I wanted to. I would probably be greatly surprised If I did find out there would be little I could do to alleviate the particular mental distress of the writer.

Again, a few weeks ago, I got a letter with two holy pictures from one who calls herself 'Good Catholic Mother.' How does she know she's a good Catholic mother? Somebody else will decide that for her at an unexpected date. Anyway, good Catholic mothers or good any kind of mothers do not write anonymous letters. Of course the alleged 'Catholic mother' may be nothing more than a small, jealous little man.

Anonymous letters have broken up homes and will continue to break up homes. They have broken hearts –

and I know what I'd like to break if I got hold of some of the writers.

Maybe there is an anonymous letter writer reading this. For the love of God, cop on to yourself and cut it out! You're just as bad as a hit-and-run driver and you deserve nothing but contempt.

At first these letters upset my wife and I to no end and kept us awake at nights wondering what I had done to arouse such a loathsome form of antagonism. But now we take them in our stride and whenever one of us opens a letter the first thing we do is to look at the end of it for a signature. If there isn't a signature, it goes straight into the fire, and what we don't know doesn't trouble us. I think this should be the procedure with everybody who opens a letter. Begin at the end and destroy it if the author hasn't the courage to sign his name. There is no justification for filth-mongers who publish pornographic muck but at least they are human enough to admit that they do so for money. What sort of reward does the writer of the anonymous letter reap. I don't know, but I do know that they turn the stomachs of all men and women who have an ounce of decency.

But I digress, so let me return to the world of the theatre for a while. Micheal Mac Liammoir said that the theatre is an evil place for those who do not belong. Any place is an evil place for those who do not belong. I do not belong to the theatre, at least to the metropolitan theatre which claims tradition with portfolio. Anybody can belong to the rural theatre. It is not an evil place and nobody should try to tell us that the rural theatre is not truly international. Shakespeare was a country-boy and so was Yeats. So was T. C. Murray and so was Lorca. But we must keep the rural theatre free from too much metropolitan influence and let it develop its own character. In many aspects, it's still a sprawling adolescent but not for long because the theatre is experiencing the pangs of re-birth in rural Ireland. It is taking a strange shape, but the stranger the better, and the more independent of outside influence the better. Gone are the days when a bit of fishing gut had to be tied to the legs of an actor to remind him that it was his turn to say something, or to stop him from saying too much.

Gone are the days, too, when forgotten plays had to be unearthed for last-minute productions. New plays by country-boys are springing up like mushrooms all around us. Maybe some of them are crude and clumsy but it must be remembered that you cannot build, a new native drama in a generation. The rising generation should bring the harvest of plays which the theatre needs to give it life and vitality and exuberance, to give it hilarity and lunacy and bustle because these are the things that a rising generation has in abundance.

But where does all this leave me? To-morrow, I'll be here in the kitchen, or maybe I'll walk down the Feale River to see what way the water is. I'll meet an oul' poacher I know well and we'll have a smoke and he might say: 'How're the plays goin', John?' and I'll say: 'Fine! Fine, thanks!'

Then, maybe, he'll shake his head wisely and say: 'Some people are not like more people at all!' and I'll say: 'You never spoke a truer word!'

I'll walk further down the river where I wrote a poem

shortly before I went to England for the first time: –

> *Oh, my love, my first love, lie down here beside me*
> *Oh, my love, my dear love, oh sweet love betide me.*
> *Lie still in my arms, do not moan, love, or tremble*
> *The wild doves are sleeping upon the green bramble.*
>
> *All over Feale River the shadows are falling*
> *And deep in Shanowen the vixen is calling.*
> *The sweet night is young, love; the night is forever*
> *And shadows are falling all over Feale River.*
>
> *I would fly like a bird with white wings in the air*
> *Or swim the salt water far off into Clare;*
> *Come close, love, come closer, look deep in the pool, love,*
> *Was ever love-making so tender or true, love.*
>
> *Oh, my love, my first love, the salmon are leaping;*
> *Lie still, my hard heart, my beloved is sleeping.*
> *The sweet night is young, love: to-night is forever*
> *And grey breaks the dawn on the banks of Feale River.*

Summer time is tourist-time, and we get our share of them down here. We get every denomination that God put into the world.

Sometimes we get honest-to-God genuine people and other times we get smart Alecs who know the answers to everything except, maybe, what's wrong with themselves.

Some times we get visits from fly-by-night reporters, attached to no particular paper, but people really on the make for something juicy or something that will show Ireland in a false but derogatory light. Most accredited journalists are genuine and conscientious, but the lies the other gazebos tell are enough to drive a man to distraction.

I remember last summer two English newspaper men from a certain English daily were on their way home from Inch after the filming of 'The Playboy'. They called in for a jar to break the journey. They spent an hour over one drink but they missed nothing that went on about them. After a while a tinker-woman, well and truly scattered, with a baby in her arms, came in looking for a drink. I refused her and she became annoyed. My two boys said nothing, but they were so interested that I asked myself: 'What's going through the noodles of those two scandal-knackers!'

The tinker-woman departed when she had conclusively proved my illegitimacy. The gentlemen of the press said nothing. After a half hour of staring, they departed. That night at about twelve o'clock the 'phone rang. The name of a certain newspaper was announced. Would I speak to them. Of course I would.

'Tell me,' the voice asked, 'is it true that you, who wrote 'Sive', refuse to serve tinkers in your bar any more?'

'Nonsense!' I said. 'I served two of your reporters here this morning!'

Needless to say there were no more questions but they got me back afterwards. One night as I was going on the stage of a certain Dublin hall to make a curtain speech, a few non-fans told me what I could do with myself. This was before I opened my mouth. Naturally I reiterated by telling them what they could do with themselves. Pandemonium broke out but order was restored after a while and the evening concluded in a relatively happy manner.

Some days later some kind soul posted my wife a copy of the English newspaper. Inside were the headlines: '*Naughty Word Author Says 'I Was Drunk'*' There followed an imaginary interview with a staff reporter of the paper. The truth is that I spoke to nobody that night except my oul' segocias in the front row who were probably a good deal drunker than I was and told me off just for the fun of it.

Somebody suggested I should sue this paper but that would be just what they wanted. I got my own back some time ago when I sent a representative of the paper to West Kerry after an imaginary forty seven-foot whale which had been washed ashore there.

About the tourists. As I said, we get smart Alecs, but then the world is made up of two kinds of people – those who make things easy for everyone, and those who don't.

A goodly number of customers frown at the not too up-to-date condition of the bar and some ask if there is a lounge. It's the way they ask that annoys me, because you know from the cut and the gameze of these characters that 'twas far away from lounges they were reared. I haven't got a lounge and I've no notion of getting one. It might keep Dickeen Roche out and I don't think old Jack Duggan would approve or for that matter any of the lads. We have no Television in the bar. It was outvoted by nineteen votes to nil.

There is nothing wrong with being a publican. Saint Paul, in his Epistle to the Corinthians, said: '*Take a little wine for thy stomach's sake and for thy frequent infirmities*' and will you tell me how better can men live than by executing the behests of the great Epistler.

It seems to annoy certain sensitive literati that a common publican should have the temerity to write plays, but sure anybody can write a play if they want to badly enough. Jack Duggan has spoken of writing a play about nothing but porter. And Dickeen Roche said the other night: 'I think I'll write a play myself and sell the rights to Hollywood. I'll be sittin' back here then with long red plucks on me like a rooster and a huge white belly like a harvest frog, or I'll be like John B. there with a pub of my own and plenty of potstill whiskey to last me out the rest of my life.'

Any fool can write a play if he listens. The world around us, particularly the rural world, is alive with singing language and fabulous characters, but there's little respect for the country poet any more. Ballygologue, a small place near Listowel, boasted nine poets and every one of them wrote a poem about Ballygologue:

'In all my life a soldier, I was never drilled but once
In the Kerry Militia barracks under Corporal Dinny Bunce,
And he said 'You drunken soldier' and he tapped me on the poll
'I'll have your name, your leg is lame, knocked offa the Munster roll;'
'So off to hospital I was sent and on a hommock laid
Because I couldn't keep up the step with the Ballygologue Brigade.'

It isn't so hard to create when you're reared on stuff like this. Every townland and parish is vibrant with the ballads of our departed poets. They're there waiting to be adopted and woven into the fabric of a living theatre, a theatre which is forcing its way upward and outward.

And look at the characters all around you, the genuine, earthy, soft-spoken wits who surround you. It's only beginning.

At night, when I open the back gate for Dickeen Roche, who has been wheeled down the backway – in teeming rain, maybe – by his two daughters, I am reminded that life is worthwhile.

'How's things to-night, John?' Dickeen might ask.

'A touch of a cold in the head, Richard!' I might reply.

'Ah, thanks be to God, we have our health!' Dickeen is sure to say. He might go on then before we pushed him into the back kitchen: 'And how're the plays goin'?'

'Not too bad! Not too bad!'

'I'll wipe ye all out shortly, when I've my own play finished.'

'What's it about, Dick?'

'Canaries... an', maybe, I'll have a few herrin's in it, an' maybe I might have a couple o' pigeons in it, if I get the notion.'

Into the kitchen then, and the affairs of the world are put in order. Things are quiet towards the end of Autumn, and Winter sees only the old reliables sitting around the fire in the back kitchen. There's always a hopeful air because Spring is just around the corner. Outside the normal hopes, hates, loves and jealousies of the average community make life worth living but all these things are surface and underneath lies the massive natural dignity of mankind.

The Feale River runs unendingly in a sleepy halfcircle about the town and in the distance the outlines of the Stacks Mountains add to the sanity of the scene and I hope and pray that I will never have to leave these haunts again for the bones in a man accustom themselves to the humours of his native winds and breezes.

Midnight and the glasses are washed, the bar empty and the fire fairly bright. I'll do a bit of writing to-night: get out the oul' copy-book and begin with 'Act I, Scene I,' and 'Action takes place...' etc., and God only knows what way the whole thing will finish up.

Mary and the boys are asleep in their beds and the fire crumples, and there are

> *'Faces I remember*
> *From June days long ago*
> *Faces of cold November*
> *Old men I used to know*
> *And memory embraces*
> *Faces of March and May*
> *From half-remembered places*
> *Sad ones and strangely gay*
> *Soft innocents unsullied*
> *Gentle, cleft of schin,*
> *And faces I have bullied*
> *With sleight of mind to sin.'*

A man's conscience is a terrible judge and few of us can examine the past without blushing. Man is the only animal that blushes, Mark Twain said, and the only animal with reason to blush. Remember that, when you feel like passing judgment.

I had better conclude.

Up to this stage of my life mine is not a very exciting story but, like most people, I have enjoyed talking about myself.

Good luck and God bless!

www.ingramcontent.com/pod-product-compliance
Ingram Content Group UK Ltd.
Pitfield, Milton Keynes, MK11 3LW, UK
UKHW021844130125
453507UK00010B/176

9 781781 179116